Untimely Ghosts

Murderous Accusations from the Tomb

By

Yda H. Addis

Yda H. Addis

"All houses—all insensate objects—in time become more or less strongly charged with the magnetism positive or negative, of the people who use them."

From Yda H. Addis's *Shadows and Voices*

Introduction

No rattling of chains, nor strange noises, and what about flashes of light, mysterious odors and odd breezes— Never! Not even a lonely bell ringing from nowhere or a musical instrument playing past the edge of time, all nixed. Instead the nineteenth-century American writer of ghost stories, Yda H. Addis, shows her readers occurrences of the murdered dead returning to the world of the living. They rise up from their catacombs not for campy theatrics of dragging shackles and scaring the bejesus out of people, but they return for a purpose: for justice, to let the murderer be known.

Addis shapes her stories around the murderer's inducements to take a life. Greed and lust are the major themes. When out of control these strong emotions may create sudden bursts of rage, or homicidal urges to protect one's evil deceptions, and then there is the premeditated killer. In that case, the desire to obtain money, especially if one's rich sickly wife has little time left among the living; the question arises: should the greedy and matrimonially discontent husband hurry up the inevitable to obtain her money and his freedom?

The question answered when the newly widowed husband, "Roberto Cantera, ... imposing, more impressive than ever with his rotund figure, his round, close-clipped head, his brown face, like the face, ... of some plump Hindu idol, and his well-fed and complacent prosperous air" who soon after the death of his wife began to court a young American lady.

La niña *Americana*, as she was called, was preparing in her dressing room to meet with Cantera. When she stepped away from her dressing table then "looked back at the mirror, and there was the strange woman's face, as plain as ever." The young woman screamed "the mirror on my dressing table; the thing is bewitched!"

When Cantera and the house servants entered the room, he recognized the face in the mirror. "From the image we at first see like a reflection, the semblance grows into relief from the surface of the mirror and detaches itself there from. Somewhat of misty outline appears, and, more swiftly... becomes the well-defined and apparently tangible figure of a woman, who floats or glides over and stands at the side of Roberto Cantera. He turns and looks into her eyes, stern, piteous, accusing, and then, with a cry like the tones of nothing human, he throws his arms aloft and falls to the floor in terrible convulsions" in *Side Lights of Mexican Society*.

From premeditated murderer for money to non-requited love killings, it is those who turn into monsters when their desires are not met. Addis points to these individuals who become vile executioners when rejected; thus, sending their love interest into an untimely grave.

However, in a particular story, Addis noticeably deviates in character and motive for murder. For the late nineteenth-century reader—bondage, an uncommon subject—whereby the sub-missive female is restrained and unable to protect herself from the hands of the dominant person is a scary situation. Intensifying the scenario Addis has the dominate male leaving the "love" scene in search of a priest in order to bring him back to the setting. One could conclude to perform a marriage (now that's a chilling thought) or was it something else?

The story takes place late at night; the priest, Friar Lorenzo, is walking to the church on a lonely street in Mexico City when he is followed and then stopped. He is requested to go along with the individual to his home. At first the cleric refuses with "spare me, I pray, your worship. I am old and feeble; since noon of yesterday I have kept vigil, and flesh and spirit alike are fainting." But his pursuer insists, the old cleric acquiesces and follows. He enters a large old Spanish style mansion, and is guided through a hallway into a darkened room. There an individual lay still. "The friar drew back with a start and a shiver when he had bent over the woman; for she was fast bound to the rude bed, made moveless by harsh cords that held her beautiful naked arms outstretched by her sides, and lashed her feet, too, closely. An observer of more worldly knowledge than Friar Lorenzo would have guessed that she had been borne hither from some scene of gala and rejoicing, for on her delicate wrists, and on her exquisite neck, and in the soft masses of her dark hair, blazed splendid jewels; and the zone of her corsage, showing above the coverlet, roughly wrapped around her, showed that the stuff of her garb was of exceeding richness."

The Friar speaks to the woman, but sooner than naught the male orders the priest to stop, then physically removes the cleric from the room and puts him into the street in Addis's tale of *An Unshrived Ghost*.

With this strangeness and the other alarming scenes, Yda H. Addis's *Untimely Ghosts* takes apart reality in order to haunt and to entertain the reader.

—Sterling Saint James

Contents

Shadows and Voices

The Wraths of Two Lovers and the Ghost of a Perfume

None had ever spoken of the house as haunted. It was so very commonplace of aspect that surely even the most imaginative mind might fail to connect with it aught of romance. A great brick barn of a house, square-built and stiff, it was; its shutter-less windows plumb and prim; its angles and lines all parallel and quadrilateral; its long piazza across its entire front certainly the very ugliest that was ever built of porches. Yet lovers had lingered there, and its echoes had held words as sweet as any hallowed ground of song or story. Ay, it even seemed to me, who then knew naught of its history in the truer inwardness of the affair, that the dingy brick walls were pallid with a wanness like the ashes of burnt-out passion. But then I—so they say—am whimsical and full of fantastic fancies.

We took the house. First when it was built had lived there the Ransomes; and they had not seemed to prosper. Constant Ransome had had an affair, none knew of just what nature, with the younger Earle, and she had been ill very long, and more than nigh unto death, while the Ransomes lived here in Sotoma. Then Fred Franck, the owner, a young German, hale and hearty, had brought a wife from among the robust stock of his native Pennsylvania, to occupy the dwelling his own hands had reared. The child born to the Francks within the year fell, a babe of six months, from its crib to the floor—just such a tumble as many a youngster gets, and shows not even a bruise for it. But Georgie Franck, up till then a great, rosy boy, full of engaging perversities and animation, from that moment peaked and pined, in mind and body, until he sat all day dumb, helpless, and imbecile. His wholesome German mother bent and broke under the affliction; and great, clumsy, honest Fred took to drink, and one day, stupid with liquor, fell from a scaffolding and never breathed after he reached the ground. Another newly married couple succeeded the Francks; within the year they were seas apart, divorced and miserable. Of the next tenants, ranging from a son of thirty down to the eighth child of five years, three died, two sons came to grief, domestic or financial, and one daughter went to the bad from a family of irreproachable antecedents.

—

2

The lesser ills and calamities seemed to have gathered here innumerably, and disease of some nature had been an ever-present guest.

Not a desirable record for a dwelling place. But we heard none of these ominous tales until long after, and the agent, noting no doubt my favorable impression by the mention of the Ransomes as former occupants, dwelt upon their satisfaction with the house, and the long stay they had made therein.

"But Miss Ransome was always ill there, was she not?" my father asked, dubiously.

"Miss Ransome's malady was constitutional—hereditary," the man replied, and I substantiated his assertion.

"I don't see why it should stand six month vacant, with houses as scarce and dear as they are here," my father persisted.

"Why not inspect the premises, at least?" the agent answered; "I will afford you every facility, and indeed, I would like to have your professional verdict, in any case."

There seemed no reason in the world why we should not be perfectly safe and comfortable there domiciled. Lower Sotoma lay in the natural drain of the valley, and malaria sometimes bred there in consequence; but the brick house was built on the hillside, from whose solid granite its cellar and cistern were blasted. This hygienic superiority, the high ceiled, airy rooms, the clean white walls, and manifold conveniences, reassured and decided us.

On either side of the hall was a large square front room, and, during the first month of our occupancy, I took for my chamber that on the left side. Then, for a caprice, I chose to exchange into the opposite apartment, which was constructed as one of the pair of parlors, communicating by folding doors. As our lack of area required the rear room also for a sleeping apartment, I utilized wall space by setting my bedroom sofa before the locked doors.

Lying on the couch one mid-afternoon, I dropped my book of travels, and quickly turned my face from the wall, as I heard a voice close beside me, breathing softly into my very ear:

"My darling, I am here."

It was the voice of a man—young and full, and withal very fond. An answer came, as unmistakable and distinct as if I myself had spoken:

"I thought you would not come; it rains furiously."

"Do you think the rain would keep me from you?"

Not very original speeches; neither brilliant nor startling; but uttered against my cheek, in a place where I was quite alone, while the rain dashed wildly outside, the matter induced sensations far from commonplace. I own that

I was startled. I hastily went up the stairs and kept my mother in close company until our merry crew came home, and their jollity modified my fear. But from that time on I led a life of continual apprehension, and consequent misery. To be alone was to be haunted! At first only my own chamber was the scene of my suffering. Then, I sat one night on the long front gallery, watching a storm-cloud rolling over the valley from the eastern mountains. I remember that I was pondering a newly developed theory of electric currents and its treatment in a magazine I had been reading, when I noticed that, by the lightning's glare, the blossoms on a vine on the porch appeared of a color complementary to their natural hue. I was sure that I had made a discovery. The whole firmament blazed with the wide flashes that brought out every vein and line of the folded buds. Eager to investigate the phenomenon, I fixed an intent gaze upon the wreathing climber, and awaited the next flash. It came, and it showed me, against the leafy background, a young man sitting on the railing—a light, boyish figure, with a grace that was all its own. There was no possibility of mistake. I noted every detail; every curve of thick soft hair, and fine chiseling of his delicate, dark face. Not one, nor ten, but many fire-flashed showed me this, and more. The stranger's gaze was bent on a pair before him in the porch. Constant Ransome was crouching on a low seat, with her head laid on her father's knee. I knew every feature of that haughty young face, every lap of the long, drooping braids of hair that fell to her as she sat. And my own father's countenance was hardly more familiar to me than the father of my friend. A head like an Arab sheik, with flowing gray beard, the eye and the beak of a hawk, with a skull-cap crowning his bald brow, Mr. Ransome was a striking figure, even a handsome one; but his bland and cruel face had always filled me with distrust. His bright blue eyes gleamed coldly now through the lurid illumination, and I heard his voice—genial to the sense, galling to the soul:

"I think we must say good-night, my boy, the storm comes in apace, and I fear you will be caught in its might if you stay with us later."

The young man stood up, and I saw a look of anger sweep over his face, and I saw him loose his hand from the clasping hand of Constant Ransome that had stolen out to detain him.

"Ay, it will be a Tam O'Shanter sort of night," he said. "I will act upon your hospitable advice, Mr. Ransome. Good-night, Miss Ransome; I wish you happy dreams."

As to one in a vision, the next lightning showed me the porch vacant. My mother came to the door and spoke:

"Sylvia, what madness! Sitting here in the damp night air, sensitive as you are to a chill! Is that your brother at the gate? Ralph, why do you not come in?"

A shape stood at the gateway, where the hall light streaming down the walk, cast a penumbra. But another moment and the night was empty; and through the roll of thunder and the dash of rain I seemed to hear the voice of Constant Ransome:

"Ah, Will! Come back!"

From that night on my soul was tortured with specters of vision, as well as wraiths of sound, as day by day the love-drama of my school-days friend was reenacted before me. Sometimes I only heard the Voices. And now I knew why, from the first, the woman's speeches in all cadences had had the echo of some beloved tone, long unheard and well nigh forgotten. But the Voice of the man! Ah me! I think not many women can have listened to a wooer like this incorporeal lover in my chamber—the cry of passion at once so strong and so tender, so ardent and so pure, as this.

But sometimes I saw Shadows. It might be that rising from my cushions, or turning to look over my shoulder. I saw a dark and tender young face bending down to mine with love-light in its eyes; perhaps in the hallway, crouching on the lower stairs, or in the long porch, I encountered the graceful shape of Constant, and a slender, boyish form beside her, instinct with pride and fondness. And ever and anon the gliding figure and the vulture face of my friend's father came between the pair. The right-hand front room seemed always, however, to be the focus of manifestation—the central nucleus from which the forces emanated.

I can not begin to express the suffering these things caused me. It was in vain that I set myself to reason upon the subject; the matter exceeded the limits of rationality and logic. I dared not carry my trouble to my family. By their sturdy practicality and incredulous horror of everything irregular or savoring of the supernatural, I would have been pronounced a victim of dementia. And yet I knew that I was not insane. Distressed beyond measure in mind, and, by inevitable reaction, in body, I was indeed; but in no slightest degree was my reason impaired.

Among the acquaintance I had formed here in Sotoma was a young man in whom I was much interested; that is to say, as regards the purely intellectual side of my nature. He was the very last man whom I would have dreamed of making the object of a tender passion; indeed, I think women like myself, of introspective and metaphysical tendencies, are mostly liable to become enamored of men who are splendid physical types merely, and devoid of high intellectual or spiritual attainments. Mr. Harper was a slight, serious young man, with a pale, grave face, his converse gad for me the charm of absolute congeniality, and I always hailed his coming. He came to the house one evening while I was under this stress of conflict with the strange demonstrations that were wearing my life out. We both had been reading Spinoza, and that was the theme of our entire discourse. We had been holding animated and somewhat abstruse discussion, when, in reply to an observation from Mr. Harper, I found myself repeating a poem of singular power and melody. The verses were exquisitely phrased and faultless in construction; the sentiment, psychological and speculative, was thoroughly pertinent to our motive. But the thing which was remarkable was that, when I had finished, I was entirely at loss for my familiarity with the lines. Not only was I ignorant of their author, but I had no remembrance of having acquired them—I could refer back to no previous knowledge of them.

"In what publication did that clever conception appear?" Mr. Harper asked, with some interest.

I laughed. "I am not quite sure it has appeared at all; I am beginning to believe I am an unconscious poet, and that I have written 'that clever conception' in a dream. I have not the faintest recollection of having read it ever, and yet you know that I am rather an authority on placing these things to proper credit."

Mr. Harper looked at me curiously. "Did you ever happen to know a Miss Ransome?" he said, a little dryly.

"Constant Ransome? Indeed, yes! We were at school together for years."

"Would you say she was capable of imposing as her

own spontaneous effort the production of another person, or even one which she had previously elaborated?"

"Never!" I averred, hotly. "She was the most scrupulously honest person I ever knew; besides, she had no need! She could always write off-hand the brightest and most finished things! Oh, she could have been famous if she had only had a little more self-confidence!"

"Well," said Mr. Harper, slowly, "Miss Ransome lived, as you perhaps know, here in Sotoma—in this very house, in fact. And here, one night, in presence of myself and—another, she wrote those verses. They deal with our text on that occasion; indeed, she wrote as we talked, while taking her part in the symposium. It struck me at the time that the girl had, as you say, a spark of divine fire, but she laughingly disclaimed any merit in the lines, and gave me them without copying, to be used in a paper I was preparing for a certain magazine. Circumstances prevented its completion, but I have never shown the verses. I have them now," he continued, taking a note-book from his breast; "imagine my surprise at hearing them from your lips."

I took the paper. It was written in the clear, nervous hand I knew, and ran, with the difference of a word or two, exactly as I had quoted.

"Now," said Mr. Harper, "the question is, how did you know these verses?"

"How did I know them? I have not seen Constant Ransome for five years, nor heard from her directly in that time. How could her words have become known to me?—unless—oh, Mr. Harper, you will think me mad! You will shrink from me in contempt—but I am going to tell you a strange, strange story! I must tell some one!"

And then, without farther prologue or preface, I told him of the ordeal I had suffered from the impalpable apparitions about the house.

"They are intangible; they are certainly unreal," I concluded. "But it is equally certain that they are not pure hallucination. For, as I have told you, various members of the family have seen the Shapes, but always vaguely, and under such condition as to be mistaken for a material Presence—one of the natural tenants. I have not dared undeceive them. I have seen and heard—I know not what. There must be some explanation—but how to find it! This mystery, this nervous train, is killing me!"

"The tension certainly has told upon you sadly," Mr. Harper said, with much evident compassion. "You should have spoken before. Often to tell one's trouble is to begin its cure. Now, I have a theory. I happened upon it years ago, and it seems to apply here. Let us see if it satisfies you. You had known Miss Ransome long and well; you were intensely en rapport with her. You come here to what you know to have been her home for some time. All houses—all insensate objects—in time become more or less strongly charged with the magnetism positive or negative, of the people who use them. This force, the effect of a complete change in your climatic and atmospheric surroundings, and modifying influences on your physical conditions—these act together upon your nervous organization. Yours is the superlatively sympathetic temperament, sensitive to the most minute variations of the psychical barometer, we may say. Here, in brief, you have your nature, primed to the highest degree of receptive susceptibility. Now for the agent. You know and I know the power of Miss Ransome's character. She is an incarnate Will. She has been dying for years; nothing else has kept her alive but that same indomitable resolution that would not let her yield a hair's breadth in her ill-fated love affair. Ah, you start! You were not aware how much I knew of that history! I was the boy's sole confident. I did my utmost to serve as mediator, and might have succeeded, but for the singular circumstance that Miss Ransome had infected her lover with her own unbending firmness."

He paused. His face always pale had grown ghastly. His benignant eyes were wide and strained.

I thought I understood these signs of suffering. This man was my friend. He had sorely pitied my strait, and had wrenched open his own wound in the endeavor to relieve my affliction. And yet, with women's inborn feline cruelty, I would not deny myself the sight of his throes when I stabbed him anew. Ah! me! Are we all made to rend the hand that helps us?

"It was hard," I said, softly, sweetly as women do speak when they strike: "was it not hard for you to try to make their peace—to reunite their hearts?"

He looked at me, that noble, generous soul!—looked straight into my face, that was hateful, I knew, with this devilish, mocking smile.

"How—hard—God—only—knows! And yet, as He hears me, I never faltered."

$\mathcal{P}$art 2

$\mathcal{H}$e bent his face upon his hand, and sat silent so long that Bebée, my pet fawn, unfolded her slender legs in the corner where she was crouched, aroused by the cessation of speech, and came to lay her pointed muzzle on my knee, looking up into my face with the mute questioning of sensitive dumb creatures. My companion laid a caressing hand on the animal's dappled coat, when finally he raised his eyes. I could not help thinking with what fondness his hand would have rested on the head of a woman he loved; how softly he would touch the cheek of a child. "To resume," he said, with the tension of lips that bespeaks determination opposed to disinclination. "After the estrangement between Miss Ransome and her lover, what is more natural than that her whole being should concentrate in her regretful memories. That strong, tenacious nature, brooding over the past, reviews in turn every phase and scene of the episode; and re-living those days herself, her personality outreaches space, and her spiritual presence returns here to fill its old place. What wonder that you have re-lived with her those old experiences? You are filled with the very essence of your friend's existence. You may even be the vehicle of her occupation. Who knows? For we realize, you and I that there are many relations between mind and mind, and between mind and matter, occult now, but which will one day be classified, and even regulated, as absolutely as are actions of the exact sciences."

Were these the far-fetched and illogical conclusions of a visionary of a mystic? Or did the rational and practical thought and studious foresight speak in this soothing, prophetic tone? I can not tell. I only know that, theory or illusion, the suggestion brought me comfort.

With something of my old impetuous eagerness, I sprang up, and drew Mr. Harper across the entry to the threshold of my own room, and impulsively threw open the door.

"Show me," I cried, "where Constant used to sit—

where stood her favorite chair. I believe that what you say is true, and I want data to pursue the thought. I am no longer afraid."

"Her seat was often on a sofa that stood where yours stands," he answered; "those doors were cut through since. She sat there for the most part; or in an easy chair just where the hassock lies. Ah!" he grasped my hand, with a painful, sudden force; "that scent! Do you use it as well as she?"

In the days when I had first known Constant Ransome her garments and her books had been always faintly redolent of a delicate perfume that I have never otherwise encountered. As we grew to confidential terms, she had told me how the rare order was the tincture of a un-spissited gum brought back by her uncle from early travels in the Levant. She had offered to share with me the precious essence; but it is a whim of mine that a woman should limit herself to the use of one sole perfume; and it suited my fancy to think of this Oriental fragrance as pertaining solely to the employment of my friend. So I had won her promise to make to not other the generous offer I refused. And while we stood there that exquisite aroma began to fill the air, faint at first, almost imperceptible, then more and more abundant, as if in full measure shaken out from an ample censer. Some effect this had, doubtless upon our senses. I felt a curious sensation of languor for a moment. Then, gazing into my chamber, I awakened with a start. The room seemed empty, but for the scattered débris of a dismantled apartment. The folding doors had given place to a blank wall, and Constant Ransome stood midway of the floor. She was cloaked and clad in traveling garb. Her face was wan, and set, and stern. Her eyes were turned towards us, but blankly, as if unseeing. She raised her hands toward heaven.

"Of, God!" she cried; "if to me descends our fatal gifts of curses, I pray Thee to wreak here the vengeance of my wrongs. Let a shadow of sin and sorrow rest on this house. In this room, where so much of happiness and so much misery has been mine, may none be happy. Dissension and hate come between lovers who meet within these walls; and if a child be born here, may agony and evil be its inheritance."

There was no frenzy in her voice, no passion in her face; only an earnest and deadly determination. That awful relentlessness horrified me. I remember Mr. Harper's sharp alarmed call to my mother before I swooned away. Then I remembered no more until I opened my eyes in my own room, where the subtle eastern perfume was still sweet and heavy. It was far in the night; a lamp was burning dimly on the mantel-board, and by its rays I saw my mother and one of our neighbors, a good, plain woman, whose kindnesses were shown by every sick-bed. With her good, broad, common face, her kind, fat voice, and her strong soft arms, Mrs.

Polson, seemed to me the typical nurse. She should have been professional instead of a volunteer. She was droning some recital to my mother in a monotonous, somniferous tome that was soothing rather than disturbing. With my senses still torpid from my swoon, I had listened for some moments with the ears of flesh before my perception took heed that the worthy woman was giving history of our dwelling's record, and its ill repute in the neighborhood.

"An' I'd take Sylvy out o' here," she was saying now. "I'd take her into another room just's soon's the law'd allow. I shouldn't dare to sleep in here! Why, everything happens in here! It was right there in that corner that Georgie Franck fell and crippled himself, an' his mother died' most on the very same spot. An' I've helped lay out three of the Slade children in here, inside of a month. But the worst of the lot was that morning that I come in the door just in time to see Wilkes Shelby knock his wife down. An' there she laid bleedin' just where Sylvy's bed is, an' he up and left, and went East with Anna Gay. Oh, I tell you, Mis' Tracy, I wouldn't have this room for a hundred dollars!"

That was the last I heard before I drifted away into delirium. Refractory to the influence of medicine, unconscious of the alarm of my family through those long days and nights of seeming stupor, I was in reality full of the most intense mental activity. I seemed to live a two-fold life. I was myself the compassionate friend to whom all the inwardness of the sad history was laid bare; regretful and full of sympathy, but impotent for intervention. And I was the girl herself, instinct with the thrill of a mighty love, and maddened by the misfortune that attended that hapless passion. With her I doubted and feared when its force first swayed her, resisting with all the startled recoil that was characteristic of Constant Ransome's almost fiercely vestal nature. With her I yielded in reluctant relenting when her debonair young lover's pleading won her forebodings over to dreams of security in a happy future. It was all so clear; I grew to understand so well in that abnormal condition. The intentions and the motives of all the players in that little drama unfolded themselves to my perception as by clairvoyance. The little rift of discord that grew into deadly distrust and hopeless division between lovers was hardly less plain than the avarice and covetousness that prompted Mr. Ransome to destroy his daughter's happiness. How well he knew his child! Who else would have suspected that under her self-contained air of confidence lay smoldering the hottest fire of jealousy that ever consumed a woman's heart? Even her young lover had found fault with her for her lack of the cursed trait that separated them.

"If I could only make you care!" I had heard the Voice of his Shadow say, long back in my first mediumistic hearings. "If I married another woman to-morrow, you would not lift a hand to hinder—you are so indifferent! So cold! You don't know how to love—for love is always jealous!"

And the girl had only smiled in her shy, proud reticence. But her father had known better. He had fanned with a steady purpose that latent spark, until it had blazed into a wild, devouring flame; his carefully shown seeds of suspicion and distrust had sprung up and borne bitter fruit.

From this strange, unwonted life, wherein my frail body had seemed to be possessed in turn by diverse turbulent spirits, I awoke once more, with a strange sense of peace. I heard the rain beating through the vines outside; and coals dropping on the hearth in the parlor across the hall; and my mother's soft stir, as she moved in some office for my comfort, no doubt. I half arose from my pillow, and then I saw the form of Constant before me once again. My whole soul shrank in horror. Would she invoke again the curse that a dark tradition in her family assigned as the heritage to the eldest born of each generation? Was she so relentless? She stood, slight and tall, in long, white draperies, like the clinging folds of a night-robe. The sad, worn face of my old companion changed, and took on a look of peace and love well nigh divine. She uplifted again her hands, but now imploring, humbly.

"Oh, Father, spare the guiltless! Not even forgiveness for my sinful prayer—but lift its wicked, horrible fulfillment—

and let our gift of curses die—with me!"

Through that misty, fading figure in the doorway, I saw my mother coming from the room beyond, and I heard, at the moment, the clock strike four. Even as mother approached the bed a sense of repose came over me, a relaxation from nervous tension, and I soon slept peacefully and long.

A week later Mr. Harper was shown into the parlor where I reclined, convalescent, since my fever had gone and I was no longer a victim of apparitions. For all disturbing sights and sounds had ceased with the last apparition of Constant Ransome in my room. The metaphysician drew his chair beside my sofa.

"Are you well enough to let me annoy you with one of my perplexities," he said, when we had chatted a few moments. "It is heartless to trouble you, but Will Earle insists that I must ask you to send him what you have in keeping for him. He came in from the mountains yesterday, the wreck of his former self, and is at my house seriously ill. I'm afraid trouble has driven him to evil ways that will be his death. But he would give me no rest until I should come here. Do you understand at all what he means."

"Not in the least," I said. "Might papa take me to your house soon? I would like to see Mr. Earle. What is he like— have you his picture?"

Mr. Harper drew a photograph from a pocket-case.

"He is not much like that now, poor boy—more like its wraith."

But it was the same dark, bright, young face I knew too well.

My father came into the room with a packet in his hand. "Ah, Mr. Harper, I am glad to see you! A good, brisk tilt against your wits will do our invalid a world of good. Daughter, here is a parcel the express-man left with me for you."

And the two gentlemen engaged each other while I opened the package. There was a worn clasped book, a journal by its appearance; a few letters bearing the name of Constant Ransome, frayed by much handling; a faded rose, two pictures of Will Earle, two little rings, and a lock of silky black hair. In a separate cover were two letters addressed to myself.

MY DEAR YOUNG FRIEND [the first I opened ran]: I am sure that your tender woman's heart will bleed for the grief with which I announce to you the death of my beloved daughter and your devoted friend, Constant Ransome. She has been declining these many months. During the last few days, delirium held her in painful chains, and she seemed living over in imagination an unfortunate emotional experience whose disillusionment, I fear, told heavily in the balance against her fragility. Her strength failed rapidly, and yesterday at two o'clock A. M., we who sorrowed about her: "When the wind began to whisper and sea began to roll, Heard, in the wild March morning, the angels call."

I am my dear daughter's sole heir, and, in compliance with a request she made before delirium supervened, I forward—through your father's attorneys, as I am ignorant of your present whereabouts—the accompanying sealed package. Craving your sympathetic prayers in my profound affliction, I am sincerely yours,

AUGUSTUS RANSOME.

To Miss Sylvia Tracy, care Rand & Barker.

My early training has made the instinct of verification like second nature to me. I compared the date that Mr. Ransome gave of his daughter's death, with my last vision of Constant, pallid and frail, seemingly moribund. They were identical. I had seen her at four o'clock in the morning—she had died at two—and the difference in longitude precisely reconciled that disparity. Was not this very nearly akin to the accuracy of scientific exactitude?

And this was the last missive of my dead friend, written brokenly in feeble characters, piteously unlike the nervous, dashing script that used to be hers"

MY DEAR FRIEND: I am dying. You must remember the

malady that has been sapping my strength for years. I might have withstood its power yet a while, but I have been wounded sorely, and I have given up the fight. Suffering has not tamed my haughty spirit, not taught me feminine softness. I will not own that death has conquered me—rather I throw down my armor and challenge his fatal shaft in penance for my sin. I opened the ear of my evil pride and weak jealousy to treacherous counsel, and grossly wronged the truest, tenderest heart that ever beat. He would not forgive me—how could he? You will find the record of it all in my journal, Sylvia. I have written it there, as I have been living it all over these past few weeks, in recollection as vivid as was the dear and sorrowful reality. And when you have read it, dear, give it over to him the things I send you—poor lifeless mementoes of a love that was deep and strong, but most ill-fated. I seem to have been very near to you of late, dear friend; as this earthly body fades and perishes, I seem to have taken on something of the wide scope of outlook from the other world. I seem to have been much in your heart, and his—ay! and with one other. Sylvia, I know that you have met George Harper. Will you tell him that I know the secret! of his loyal heart, and bow my soul before his noble spirit? For the rest, I will come back from that other world—already I am half within its sway—and I will send my dear one to you, dear, for comfort. Pity him, Sylvia, for he loved and suffered much.

Keep the turquoise ring in memory of me, and give him what I have sent—it will reach him only through your hands, for my father would keep back from him even this poor remembrance from the dead. It is not sad—we two alone of all our race, and so estranged? It does seem hard to die and leave but few to mourn me—only you, and Will, and dear George Harper. I have been days writing this—my strength is failing now. Tell Will that the tress of his dear hair has never left my heart. I only sent it now to spare it profanation. Not even the sanctuary of my cold breast could save it from my father's hatred. Pray for me—Sylvia, I have been cruel, and hard, and vindictive, but I repent—I have tried to atone—good-bye—God bless you—help Will--

Constant,   May 3, 1884.

The Mysterious Woman

A Story of Strange Happenings in a Quiet Southern Town

Appeared in *The Argonaut*, March 21, 1892

When Alfred Shea and his wife went to live for a time at Platte City, the question of house-accommodation bade fair to give them some inconvenience. This was a long-settled district, and almost every family in the community had dwelt in the same house throughout the whole time of residence there. When young people married, it was either to abide in one of their respective old homes, or else, more usually, to swarm to a new establishment of their own. The people here were somewhat unprogressive; for the most part being widely inter-allied by blood or marriage with their neighbors, they and their collaterals were sufficient unto themselves, and immigration was hardly desired, certainly not courted, and no temporal provision was made for the inducement of potential settles.

It seemed to Alfred Shea that there was not a house to let in the township. He certainly had been unsuccessful in finding one within the "city" limits. His wife was newly married from a large household, reared on Southern principles and the publicity of the hotel distress and wearied her. Moreover, both were of a domestic turn, and they had the true and natural instinct of home-making.

The husband was returning from about the fiftieth unsuccessful trip in search of a house, when he was hailed by his brother-in-law, who owned and edited the local newspaper.

"Come with me," he said; "I think I have found a man who has a house to rent. I think you had better take it, although it is not large, nor near the business center."

The man they went to see was a planter from some twenty miles "in the country." The house was quite large enough, he said, for a bride and groom; in fact, it had been built for just such occupancy—for his own daughter, who did not like country life; but just before her marriage, her husband had had a good business opening in St. Louis, which of course, said her father, "suited Sis a heap better than Platte City. It's a little one-horse town, even if it is nice."

It was really not a large house, but it was large

enough. There was one spare bedroom—"so all of Betty's folks can come over, one or two at a time, to visit us," thought the young husband.

"But I though you told me," he said, "that the house had not been occupied. It shows all over it had been lived in. Not that it looks worn or dirty—except this"—he qualified as they opened the door to the kitchen—"this looks like it had been used for a charcoal-kiln."

"Well," said the owner, "I told you my daughter didn't live here, but not that no one else did. The fact is, I felt a little queer about it—about telling you that a young couple did live here—they had not been married very long, and one night the wife she upped and left her husband. He was terribly upset. I think the reason she left him was because he spoke pretty sharp to her about this very charring of this of the kitchen. She wasn't used to keeping house, he said, and she let the fat catch fire as she was frying some nut-cakes that afternoon, and it blazed up and burned out the kitchen like you see it, and he was pretty well tuckered in putting it out, and spoke to her pretty binding. He made the damage good before he left, but I never done had the kitchen done over—they's not much call for houses. I'll send the carpenters around if you say you take it."

Mr. Shea said he took it. He was sure his wife would be contended; anything would be better than to stay on at the hotel. And, in effect, she was delighted at the prospect of getting into private quarters. Within the week, the little house was modestly furnished, and they were installed. Two days after they moved in, Betty's younger brother, James, a lad of fifteen, came to make them a visit. It was very convenient to live in Platte City, for Betty's family lived only about eleven miles away, in the large town across the river, and it was very easy for them to ride or drive over to visit Betty.

James passed part of the day at his brother's office, part at his brother-in-law's store, and part in a rampage with the many lads of his age of Platte City and its environs. He was thoroughly tired at night, and went to bed early. His hosts retired some hours later, but they had been asleep some little time when they were awakened by a most insufferable yell from the youth, and the next moment he burst into their room, panting and sobbing, and bounded upon them in the bed with more force than was at all pleasant. Alfred Shea caught him and put him out on the floor again, with a vigorous remonstrance and an admonition to go back to his own bed and stay there.

"Oh, Mr. Shea!" cried the boy, "I can't! I can't! Indeed, I dassn't. Please don't ask me! It scared me so! I felt it!"

"Felt it! What did you feel? What scarred you?"

"Oh, I don't know! It was—I don't know what! It waked me—it was pulling off my covers, and when I pulled 'em back, it got up and lay down on the bed close by me—almost on top o' me!"

"Oh, pshaw! rank nonsense!" declared his brother-in-law.

But Betty piped up sleepily: "Oh, Alfred, don't scold the poor boy—dear Jem was always timid. Suppose you go and look in his room. We may have shut a dog in the house without knowing it, and it would get on the bed for warmth."

So Mr. Shea went out, with Jem holding fast to his brother-in-law's night-gown, and a thorough inspection was made, not only of Jem's room, but of all the premises. Mr. Shea looked into and under everything where even a cat might hide, but there was no dog nor cat hidden; no, not even a rat, nor so much as a cockroach or a water-bug—nothing in the world to warrant Jem's unseemly panic. The doors and windows were all fast, as they had been left at bedtime.

But nothing that could be said would induce that absurd boy to go back to his bedroom. No, he would not do it, he said; he would rather go down-town, and wake his brother, and sleep at the hotel with him. And he brought his clothes into the hall, and was actually putting them on to go away, when his brother-in-law stopped him.

"Now there's no sense in you disturbing your brother, too, and you are not to do it. I will take your mattress into our room, and let you sleep there. I had no idea you were such a baby! You ought to have a trundle-bed under your mother's big four-poster. Before I'd be such a coward!"

But Jem accepted the contumely as an offset to the solace of companionship, and went to his lowly pallet with great meekness.

The next night, in discussing Jem's inglorious fright, his sister and elder brother remembered that he had been subject to nightmares when younger, and they concluded that his excessive exertions the day before had caused a recurrence of the old trouble. That night his brother took the boy to the hotel, where he stayed three nights, seeing his sister in the day-time. And those three nights Jem heard never a whinny of even the colt of a nightmare.

Then the lad returned to sleep at his sister's, and promptly repeated his former interesting performance, with added fervor. This time nothing would dissuade him from finishing the night in the bed behind his sister, and he would not so much as peep from beneath the blankets until daylight. After breakfast, he saddled his pony and departed, and his brother-in-law said, "Good riddance! But we'll get some of the rest over, Betty, so you shan't be lonesome."

The next day, Betty's editor brother came in just before sunset, and told her that Shea had business which would keep him later than usual, and that he, Draper, had come to tell her, lest she be uneasy. The fact was that they had agreed she must never be left alone in the evening, as a good many bad negroes were thereabouts.

Brother and sister were standing near the garden-gate, watching for Mr. Shea's return. It was the gloaming; forms could be seen and dark color discerned from light, but detail could not be distinguished.

"Who can that be?" said Betty. Her brother turned toward the house, whither she was looking and saw a tallish, slender woman, in a light-colored frock, skirting the narrow gallery. She had something whitish on her head and what looked like a dark tippet over her shoulders.

Betty and her brother started to meet her, but she was before them at the steps, up which she went, passing across the porch into the house. They followed close behind her, calling, but she was out of sight, nor could they discover her.

"How sorry I am!" said Betty; "how very sorry! I suppose she went on out through the kitchen door—it was open—when she found the house not lighted, supposing we were away. Do you suppose she is deaf, that she did not hear us calling? So sorry! I would like so much to have a 'run-in neighbor" I am quite lonesome."

This hurt her brother, for he had been in Platte for some time, and felt that he ought to have made acquaintances who should call on his sister, who had been used to a deal of company. But the Platte citizens were very conservative, and distrustful of strangers as probably being "Yankees," and even "the editor" was not acquainted, except in a business way. These considerations, and the arguments they led to—for Draper deplored her isolation, and Betty stoutly protested she cared not a pin about it—turned their thoughts from the light-frocked woman, for that day; but the next morning, as the three sat on the porch, they saw the same woman walking near the gate, within the garden.

"There's your 'run-in neighbor,' Betty," said the brother; "I'll go and speak to her."

At the moment he was rising, a gun-shot sounded at the corner of the house. It must have been even with the gallery, for its flare lighted up their faces. Draper of the porch and Alfred Shea on it, both ran to the end, but nothing was to be seen of the shooter. They at once searched the place. In the back-yard were no bushes, nothing higher than some late vegetables just cropping up, and the country was open for some distance beyond. He could hardly have slipped past them into the front garden, but they nevertheless beat up the garden thoroughly. Only when they were shaking the yellow four-o'clock bushes, where they had seen her, did they remember the woman.

"Of course she made of when she heard the gun," said Draper; "who wouldn't?"

And Betty was so much alarmed by the shot, she did

not grieve for her visitor. "Oh! It's because they take us for Yankees! I just know it. Brother, do put in the Starry Flag that we are Southern."

From that time the woman was about the place almost daily. Nearly every evening—they saw her at no other time—she was either on the porch or in the garden; always the other place from where they were. Without seeming to notice them, she contrived to avoid them. Betty said she was sure it was some one who loved flowers, but who was in humble circumstances, and, on account, probably, of deficiencies in apparel, ashamed to meet people; and Betty though she slipped in to enjoy the flowers under cover of the twilight. Alfred Shea thought, but did not say, that this theory did not account for the stranger's eccentricities, such as going into the house, for instance. But he was careful not to call Betty's attention to this, lest she might share, and be alarmed by, his own suspicion, which was that the woman was one of those poor creatures, demented, yet considered—until a frenzy seizes them and they do ghastly things—"entirely harmless." He knew that very many small rural towns hold one or more such "innocents," kept out of an asylum through poverty, apathy, or mistaken affection. However, his caution inquiries led to no knowledge of any such subject in Platte City; Draper might have learned more readily, but he was gone to St. Louis on business.

About ten days after he left, Betty's mother came over for a visit. Betty was very fond of her mother; Alfred Shea, too, loved her dearly, and they spent a very happy evening, which they prolonged until an unusually late hour.

Mr. Shea was awakened from a sound slumber by a hand tugging gently at his shoulder. He sat upright: "Mother! what is the matter?"

Betty was up in an instant, and echoing his question.

"There!" said her mother, "I hoped I could arouse you without awaking Betty. Mr. Shea, will you bring my bed into this room, if you do not mind my sleeping here to-night? It is so cold—I mean so warm!—in my room, and I think you have a little breeze here. I have been so uncomfortable."

Now this was a lady who never complained; she would suffer almost any inconvenience rather than cause another person even so much—or so little—trouble as she was giving her son-in-law. He went at once to move her bed. He noticed that she did not leave the room, but went and stood with her face to the window while he effected the transfer. After they were all back in bed, he heard her shivering.

This arrangement remained in force for three or four nights, then the guest moved her bed back to the spare room. In the middle of the night Alfred Shea heard a little low cry from across the hall. His mother-in-law was a woman of lovely, mild manner, and all her demonstrations were very gentle. He knew that that faint cry from her meant as much as a shriek from other women. He threw on a dressing-gown and hurried to her. She had made a light, and was sitting up in bed. Her face was blanched, and she looked greatly disturbed.

She motioned to close the door, and then asked, in a strained voice: "Have you—have you a dog here?—a big dog—mastiff or Newfoundland."

"There is no dog here," said Alfred Shea. "I have been trying to get one to protect Betty in my absence, but have not found the kind I want, yet."

"I was quite sure it was no dog," the lady murmured to herself; "I—I knew it was not."

Side-Lights on Mexican Society

Appeared in *The Argonaut* September 24, 1888

I can not believe the evidence of my own sense of vision. I look again and again, incredulous, with strained and starting eye-balls. Then I drop the powder-puff and hand-mirror, and give a shrill, wild shriek, that goes reverberating and echoing through the corridors of this old ex-convent, and brings Solores, Dionysia, and Hermelinda flying down the stone staircase without instigation while I can plainly hear that plump old Petra, the cook, comes waddling out of her kitchen up-stairs, and hangs herself over the railing between the flower-pots, to see what has happened the niña Americana.

"*Por Dios, niña !* What is it? Have you burned yourself? Did you put out an eye? Have you pricked your finger?" Such are the only causes the simple women can assign for my alarm, since venomous reptiles or insects there are none in this whole fair valley of Mexico: and the faithful vigilance of old José María, the *portero*, precludes the idea of a thief or other intruder coming in from the street.

"No, nothing of the sort is the matter; I—I felt lonely," I said lamely, feeling assured that the whole trove of superstitious creatures would flee from the house immediately if I confess the truth; "go and ask the niña Josefita to come down here to speak to me, and at once! Tell her I am ill, and weak, and can not climb the stairs. And you stay here, Hermelinda, with me until she comes."

Josefita comes down at once, stopping midway still putting her clothes on. Her placid face is full of concern, and her mild, serene blue eyes are troubled.

"But child," she says, "What is it? I was afraid all along the excitement of these posadas gayeties would overtax your strength."

"Excitement!" I echoed, scornfully; "what is an insignificant gathering of a few dozen to my experience? I screamed, I grant you. Yes. Any woman would, I think, at looking into her mirror, while innocently putting on her powder, and seeing there reflected another face than her own."

Josefita scans me sharply, and seeing I am in earnest, she goes in a most practical manner to look into the closet, and in every nook and corner—even under the narrow, monastic iron bedstead, free as it is from all draperies that might conceal a marauder.

"Oh, that is useless, Josefita! I turned sharp about and looked over my shoulder—there was no one in the room but me. Then I looked back at the mirror, and there was the strange woman's face, as plain as ever. The mirror on my dressing table; the thing is bewitched!"

"You would have that one," remarks my hostess; "you do have the most inexplicable tastes with your notions for old fashioned styles. But, except for its inconvenience, the table there's nothing wrong with it. Your imagination has run away with you. No doubt you were composing verses, or conjuring up a fantastic story. Didn't I hear you say yesterday you need money, and must write a story? And you dreamed an incident. Furthermore, you drank pulque with guachinango for dinner, thought I have so often told you that pulque on fish will poison you."

I make no protest or demur; life is too short to waste time in idle discussion that cannot lead to a conclusion. Moreover, I begin to believe that I have absorbed something of the laissez-faire spirit of the country; so that I dismiss the subject as soon as may be, keeping close by Josefita, however, while I induct myself into such festive war-paint and feathers as are at my command, and, presently, when my hostess has also finished putting on her makeup that was interrupted by my maniac yells, we go away to the Escudos.

This is the fourth night of the posadas, but I am not tired of them. I was bothered and frightened when the mozo of the Escudo establishment brought me a thick white envelop, with its green and silver monogram, bidding me to this Christmas-season gathering, and I announced, in unqualified terms, my sentiments, and Josefita scolded me roundly. "How, then! You have declined an invitation to a house where you would have had the best of social relations? What imprudence! I know dozens of Mexican families of wealth, and of some importance, who would give their eyebrows to go there!"

"But the observances are so different here from in the United States," I protested; "I would be sure to give the wrong responses, or to stand when I ought to be kneeling. And no blunder is so unpardonable as one in connection with a religious ceremony."

Josefita laughed, as pitying my un-sophistication. "Do you think that the Escudos are so devout and pious? Wrong. These *posadas* of ours are no outpouring of saintliness; they serve as pretexts for frolic and dancing. It is too bad you have thrown away the opportunity to meet so many fine people; and then the *posadas* have the characteristic color of nationality you are always seeking. Unfortunately I can take you to no *posadas*—I have not a single invitation for them this year."

The echo of Josefita's regrets has scarcely died away when the Escudo mozo is back again, with another card, written in the first person and in a tone of kindly cordiality from my countrywoman, for the wife of Manuel Escudo is an American. "I had forgotten the question of a chaperon," she writes, "because you are an American. But you are very right to observe the conventions of the land we are in. Please, convey to your hostess the card that goes with this, and expressions of my kindest regard, and make her feel how glad I shall see her at my house with you. The carriage shall call for you at seven." It is said that Katy de Escudo has not always nestled in the lap of luxury and refinement; that she is the daughter of a washerwoman in San Francisco, in California; that even after all these years, her social blunders would be many but for the ceaseless coaching of a reduced gentlewoman, who is nominally governess at the Escudo mansion. However this maybe the daughter of a hundred earls, but could not surpass her in true thoughtfulness and kindness.

Josefita is very a little bit of a snob, but she certainly

has an eye for every material and worldly advantage, and she bridles with complacency and gratification at this opening of dialogue with the household of General Escudo. It has been not a little edifying to see her take her place among the very magnificent families of the capital, this Josefita of mine, who is only a poor boardinghouse keeper, and that in a country where labor, even on the part of a man, is regarded with considerable suspect, and where independence and self-reliance in a woman excite quite as much alarm as wonder. But Josefita is a woman in a thousand; decades in advance of her sex and race by nature, her years of self-dependent endeavor for a livelihood have developed a strong and striking individuality, which, with her gently dignity, makes a very admirable person. Then her plump, neat little figure has a certain distinction, and lends its well-chosen attire a grace aimed at vainly by not a few of the aristocratic and wealthy ladies hereabout.

In the other nights of the *posadas*, which have introduced me the cream of the social element in Mexico, these things have been growing upon me, and it is with a thrill of positive pride I follow Josefita into the glittering main sala of our hostess, and, once we are greeted by Katy de Escudo, we walk to the shrine honoring the Nacimiento. Josefita is a little bit of a beata, that is to say, a devotee, but she kneels a moment, as I do, before this picturesque altar. It is a rich and a costly display, this objective allegory of the birth of the Savior of men, and yet, in the main points, but a reproduction of the scene set forth in a thousand homes of the abjectly poor, where porters, hucksters, water-carriers, washer-women, lottery-ticket sellers, and yes! beggars themselves, impress upon their hearts the history of that divine passion by direct appeal to the responsive eye of the flesh. Here is the terraced mound of crisp green moss, banked on a firm foundation against one wall of the room; here are the twigs and branches that stand for trees; the figures of the three kings, the Magi, and shepherd with flocks and herds. There, at the apex, is the Virgin Mary and the reverent, reverend Joseph. As yet the image of the sweet Babe Divine is not visible; it will be added on the last night of the *posada*, at Christmas. In this Nacimiento of the Escudos, the trees and moss are powdered, not with flour, as in the homes of the poor, but with brilliant diamond dust; the bits of crystal bedded in the moss, imitate lakes and pools, are here of rich plate mirror; for the shred of wick floating in oil, shining through bottle of colored water, the light here glows through tinted globes from scented candles; the figures of men and angels, and all adoring creatures, are not of common clay, but of wax and costly porcelain; and the stars gleaming in the sky above, of azure silk and tulle, are all of precious gems. And yet, from the humble huts to the lofty halls, one motive rules alike, remembering the humble origin and lowly surroundings of Him whose birth is thus commemorated, that the poorer showing is nearer unto His likeness.

The procession is about to form. We are given candles, and then we form into a double file, and are marching through the rooms and corridors, singing chants, and now and then pausing to utter prayers, in imitation of the movements of the Holy Family with their search of a *posada* or lodging in Bethlehem. The Cura of Santa Brigida is with us, and he gives us his blessing, that the pampered bodies of these, his well-kept parishioners, may not be fatigued by too much devotion, and we disband to await the dancing.

Josefita and I seat ourselves modestly at one side; alone, but for a short while, General Escudo comes to talk to us, and half a score of others and Roberto Cantera, the last more imposing, more impressive than ever with his rotund figure, his round, close-clipped head, his brown face, like the face, I think, of some plump Hindu idol, and his well-fed and complacent prosperous air. His attentions to my small, obscure, and insignificant self are tonight more marked than ever. He exerts himself to the utmost. He tells me, in his soft and mellow voice the pedigree and antecedents of the families present whom I happen not to know. He has me served with refreshments proportioned to his own voracious appetite—I'm telling myself as he devours the dainties how much I abhor a glutton; and when the "flocking and dancing" begin, he insists on leading me out with a frequency that is trying. For I have a whimsical feeling that I must resemble a creature led in tow by a captive balloon; such is my ungracious and ungrateful sentiment regarding his rotund build. Yet he dances well, having the elasticity of a ball of India-rubber, and his strength of arm is great, and he whirls me very lightly. But I am a woman; and what woman, in other questions even than those of dancing, does not think more of appearance than of comfort? However Señor Cantera is determined I shall sit out few dances, and his young compatriots, it must be confused, do not betray unseemly haste in claiming me for a partner. It must be because I am a foreigner; it may be because I have the reputation of cleverness; for, sad commentary as it is on the caliber of masculine mentality, I have already found this attribute stand in the way of my popularity with young men. Whatever the cause, the fact remains that these young caballeros, in spite of their national arrogation of courteous gallantry and attention to women, neglect and slight the stranger in their midst, seemingly determined to condemn me to "eat peacock," as their saying goes. Sooth to say, I would not be sorry for this, but for the affront to my self love, for the youth of the national capital is about as graceful at dancing as the traditional grimalkin treading hot bricks. Even Roberto Cantera excels them, for Roberto Cantera is Veracruzano, and all tierra caliente people dance well.

I am destined to enjoy triumph over the *lagartijos*. Late in the evening enter a number of young foreigners, attaches of the different foreign embassies, who have been kept away by business at their respective departments. I am surprised no little to see among them a friend and countryman of mine; a young fellow of the old Knickerbocker family, who has exiled himself to Mexico on account of some family question that seemed to menace his dignity. He has passed most of his life in Europe, and his English is by no means the strong suit among four or five languages of which he speaks, yet in all his feelings and motives he is intensely American. He has some connection with the diplomatic people from home, but he is poorly paid, and I certainly never dreamed of seeing him here. Katy de Escudo must be inclined to play the part of benefactress to poor but honest Americans! Van has been as kind to me as any brother, and I—I have received his attentions with the same languid tolerance that I have of late bestowed on all things earthly.

Van looks very well in the regulation uniforms, and his slim, youthful figure and quaint, gaunt blonde face excite some attention among the señoritas.

He comes over to me directly.

"You are very pale," he says, with his air of practical admonition, as if he were nurse and physician in one; "I must order you away home to bed. You always over task your strength, if left to your own devices. But—it won't hurt you very much to waltz once with me, will it?"

In contrast with his dogmatic tone of a moment since, this change to boyish request seems very funny. I stand up laughing, and we float away in time to a languid, throbbing, sensuous Mexican danza. Van's ability in this line is heavenly, and I flatter myself that I dance in time rather neatly. Only now and then we dance as some unusually skillful couple, and I feel that no other can compare with us.

Presently I stop, and say with some of malice: "I think I will save my strength a little. I see two—five—eight of the *diplomáticos* waiting to demand an introduction, and I am convinced they are languishing to dance with the only woman in the room who does not try to revolve on three different axes at once, with three diverse kinds of motion."

And it is even so. I very soon find myself engaged ten deep to the Europeans, and chattering to them like a polyglot parrot. The lagartijos—that is to say in Spanish the dudes—reverence to the *diplomáticos*, and they too come flocking up to me in servile imitation. But I will have nothing to say to them, remembering the bad last fifteen minutes I have passed among them. My little social triumphs by-gone and I enjoy it. What woman who has been obscure and poor would not enjoy it?

But through it all, a vague oppression haunts me, and it is only now and again the vagueness changes to definition, and I remember the shock I had earlier in the evening. As a dull pain grows upon me until I am suffering almost unbearably. Van presently comes and chides me for exerting myself unduly, as he is sure I am doing, from my continued pallor, which has not been warmed by the exertion of constant dancing, nor by my full share of the champagne handed around between the dances. And finally, partly to silence his insistence that is like the voice of conscience, and partly for the comfort of speaking out my worry, I tell him of my vision. "And do you know," I say with a sudden flash of perception, "I do believe I feel it more keenly every time I look at Señor Cantera. I am very sorry, for I dislike him enough already. Oh, what an ungrateful brute I am to say so! He is goodness itself to me—almost as good as you are," I say, feelingly, for it is innate within me to offer to each and every man I know such tributes as shall grapple him to my soul with links of adamant.

Van looked viciously approving. It is not unpleasant to him to her disparagement of Roberto Cantera, whose fallow thousands can but tantalize a young man of ambition.

"But this mystery or hallucination, whichever you choose to call it, will disturb you less if you investigate it and clear it up. And if Señor Cantera seems associated with it, why not use him as a vehicle of illumination? It not infrequently happens that, when individual efforts are futile, the desired results may be obtained through even as unworthy medium."

I look at Van in blank amazement. This practical, matter-of-fact young fellow, the last on earth I would have suspected of sympathy for, or understanding of, spiritualism, mysticism, theosophy, telepathy, or any kindred subject—his discoursing thus gravely and familiarly of such matters! And, further, he plunges into such a learned disquisition on receptive media, and volitional agents, the influence of mind over mind, the power of mind over matter, and alleged supernatural effects produced by purely natural causes, that I begin to believe that the Witch of Endor and the Kentucky Devil were very commonplace and every day personages.

Van's harangue has the effect, however, and I afterward decide that was his aim in administering it—of confusing and at the same time tranquilizing me. I finish the evening's entertainment with infinite satisfaction and a flourish of trumpets, and go home so wholesomely tired that, instead of going upstairs to sleep in Josefita's room, as I had meant to do, I turn towards my own room at the mezzanine, and creep to bed thankfully and fearlessly, even going so far as to take down, even though sleepy as I am, the rebozo I had flung over the uncanny mirror.

And the next morning I am ready to laugh at my panic, and am almost convinced that what I last night saw in the looking-glass, for I knew that I did see it, was an optical delusion. I fritter away the morning lazily enough, as one does after a night's indulgence, and am rocking listlessly in my rocker when Josefita makes her appearance shortly after luncheon, accompanied by Roberto Cantera.

I am not at all pleased with her for bringing him to my private room in this fashion. There are ante-*salas* on each floor, beside the great prim, tasteless sala upstairs, where Josefita's guests, both men and women, are in the habit of receiving their visitors. She would never have dared take such a liberty with a Mexican woman. This is one of the gratuitous impertinences, all the more offensive for their matter-of-factness, that Mexicans are in the habit of showing to Americans, as to a race either ignorant, or careless, or both, of the conventionalities, the proprieties, the decencies even of life. Has some glaring adventures gone off on a little excursion with one of the ministers? She is an American—that explains it—and for all the distinctions recognized by these people, such escapades would seem to be quite the usual thing with American women of the highest classes. Do the servants address one formally as "thou," or without tipping their hats? Oh, well! It is only an American—no need to be polite.

Full of rage, as I am, I receive the two graciously enough; I am under my own roof, and the laws of hospitality are sacred. Moreover, this interview will not improbably afford me an opportunity for reprisals of that vicious-courteous nature permitted by the usages of society. Neither have I the slightest compunctions of conscience about retaliating, for I know that if Cantera should choose to vilify and malign me, on the score of this slight license, all the evidence of my austere, hard-working life and his notorious profligacy would not prevent me from being censured, condemned, shunned as an evil thing by my present associates. Even Josefita would desert me, although knowing me to be as innocent as an angel, and herself responsible for the situation. *Cosas* de Mexico! I quite understand Josefita's motives for this venture. She wishes to further a certain confidence and intimacy between us, for she is bent upon my marrying this fat countryman of hers, who can give me wealth and position.

Truth to tell, I am today more inclined than usually to lend myself to her project. My distaste of the night before has been followed by its inevitable reaction—that abnormal frame of mind in whose abyss of contrition so many women commit themselves to sacrifices for everlasting repentance. Then, the luxury that surrounded me at the home of the Escudos has had its due effect upon me, and the light of its splendor throws into blacker shadow the sordid cares that encompass me. Why should I continue to struggle with a hard and cruel world on the strength of an uncertainty? What assurance have I that the man for whom I have sacrificed some of the best years of my young life is not disloyal, rather than, like myself, a victim of treachery? Other women marry solely for money; why should I not do likewise? After all, who can answer for honor and affection, or even for worth and the stability or justice of worldly position? Who am I that I should constitute myself a judge of this man's nobility or merit, or even of his refinement? Are my standard sure to be infallible? At least he can not be worse than me in my baseness of ingratitude. So I fling consistency and principle to the winds, silencing with sophistries the protests of my soul; and I coo, and smile, and murmur, and flash with something of my old spirit, and Roberto Cantera gazes at me foolishly , and I trample down my repulsion and beam on.

In the midst of it all a *cargador* comes to the door, one of the public carriers, bearing a bouquet, a stiff and formal arrangement of the most expensive flowers in the market, mostly camellias and gardenias, and knotted across them a broad ribbon of the color of my gown I wore last night at the *posada*, which Roberto Cantera then took occasion to tell me was his favorite color. I understand, of course, and I can do no less than exclaim, rapturously. Dolores, the maid, has mislaid the only vase in my possession, and I can not possibly put these showy flowers into a jug, undoubtedly artistic, but cheap and common, into which I tuck the great bunch of violets and pansies that Van and my other friends bring me. It occurs to me that the missing vase may be behind the dressing-table, and I go to look into the corner angle.

"The humble and worthless blossoms are not deserving of being held by the hands of so much youth and beauty. I would gladly carpet with the richest flowers the path in life of one who is herself a flower," Robert Cantera is saying in his studied, grandiloquent manner.

I am between my visitors and the mirror, and I can not resist breaking into a grimace, inspired by the nauseous fulsomeness of my *pretendiente*. The face of the night before is looking back at me. I have a sensation as if my soul, rooted like a tree in my body, were being wrenched out, to its utmost fiber, with the mighty sickness that would naturally attend such a process; I behold with no particular pleasure an unusual display of pyrotechnics, and I hear the arguments of many swarms of bees in convention. I stagger a step or two toward the door, and sink down helplessly, losing consciousness, and, with the last ray of perception, I hear Robert Cantera say: "Her emotions have been too much for her. I should have more clearly manifested my intentions. She has succumbed to her suspense and anxiety."

After this, the first swoon of my lifetime, there is for me no *posada*. I return to consciousness at night fall, a little uncertain of my whereabouts, but resolutely declining to be moved from my own room, as I remember vividly the occasion of my brilliant performance, and I am resolved to see it out.

The next day I am still so uncertain of balance that I remain in bed. Van has missed me at the *posada*, and has learned the cause of my absence from Señor Cantera, who does not see fit to forego this mild dissipation because I have fainted.

Van comes to me at once, and is admitted to where I recline on a couch, attended by Dolores. Naturally I relate to him yesterday's occurrence, with all its circumstances.

"It is clear," says Van, immediately, "that the apparition in the mirror is in some way connected with Cantera; you had been thinking of selling yourself to him—forgive me!—When did you first see it? Yesterday? You approached the glass with impunity, until you did so in his presence and while you were dallying with his professions. Of what did Cantera's wife die; can you tell me?

"Pray, hush! This sounds like Bluebeard. I daresay Josefita can tell us. The poor lady died at the hacienda something less than a year ago. A short term of widowhood? By no means—a long one for a Mexican. I have known many very distinguished men here remarry within six, four, three months of their bereavement. But you are right; we will ask Josefita that question."

As if invoked by the suggestion, Josefita appears in the doorway, and she is accompanied by Roberto Cantera. This gentleman inquires for my health with so much effusion and solicitude, that one might fancy he had been mourning my swoon in seclusion and clad in sack-cloth and ashes, rather than disporting himself in all the casual gayeties of the capital. But he dislikes Van's presence, and plainly shows it, enwrapping himself in the ponderous ceremonious politeness of the country.

But Van is serene and complacent, and quite oblivious to these indications. He waxes absolutely vivacious, he, the serious, the melancholy, and rallies Señor Cantera upon his devotion to society, and me upon my hypochondriacs, indiscriminately.

Then Josefita falls into the spirit of his efforts, and in her turn indulges in good-natured raillery. "And how," she says, "do you stand now with the phantom? Is it that she will not allow you to rouge that you have lost all your bright color? Now, what a pity, since you must see a face in your mirror, that it is not the face of some hacendadito! For you, too, who like so much our dark-skinned *charros!* Never mind let the ghosts be women—the men who haunt you are certainly substantial!"

"Is the señorita a *espiritista*—a spiritualist? asks Roberto Cantera; "No, no, never disclaim your faith. Why, at one time even I had the idea to investigate those doctrines. And this is her cabinet—her *prie-Dieu* of occultism! With your permission I will see what manner of dressing table this is, that will serve such diverse purpose."

This is a very ordinary piece of furniture, such as may be seen by scores; the like is found in half the dressing rooms in Mexico. An oblong, swinging mirror, with truncated upper corners, two long, folding arms, each holding a brass socket for a candle, and the usual shelf on top, with its indentations of various shaped and sizes for putting toiletries and accessories on. I was very angry with the liberty this man was allowing himself, in action, and in taking for granted my convictions against my own denial—for, up to the present experience, I have been the most skeptical of beings as to occult supernatural manifestations. But Van checks, with a look, my expression of the displeasure he can but see depicted on my too-speaking countenance.

"Now, can you conceive, Señor Cantera," he says, "a phantom more malicious and ill-natured than on which is dancing, talking, at dinner, at mass, whenever—rather than while she is engaged in the enhancing of her natural graces for the delighting of our eyes—all unworthy that we are of such favor."

Roberto Cantera has laid his hand upon my table, on one of the two stays or braces that seem to uphold the shelf part. They are uncommonly thick, wide, and massive, but the work of Mexican joiners is mostly clumsy. As Roberto Cantera touches the bit of timber, it swings out sideways—he had touched, no doubt, a spring undiscovered by others—and I see it is dovetails out, and the hollow is full of papers.

"Where did you get this thing?" he gasps; and Josefita answers: "I bought it at a sale at the pawn shop. The manager told me it was brought in with a great deal of furniture from an old hacienda."

"Yes; Fuentes robbed me of this and other furniture, and sold it," says Cantera, brokenly; "here are some papers I missed and have been looking for—the papers of poor Concha—my dear, lost angel." He stops. Once more the mirror is filled by the face and bust of a woman—the woman I have already seen, a type of Mexican beauty, albeit worn and sickly. But—was ever the like seen of humans? From the image we at first see like a reflection, the semblance grows into relief from the surface of the mirror and detaches itself there from. Somewhat of misty outline appears, and, more swiftly than I am telling it, becomes the well-defined and apparently tangible figure of a woman, who floats or glides over and stands at the side of Roberto Cantera.

He turns and looks into her eyes, stern, piteous,

accusing, and then, with a cry like the tones of nothing human, he throws his arms aloft and falls to the floor in terrible convulsions.

Josefita and Van, all full of horror, bend over him. I do not touch him. I realize now what I have felt, but refused to countenance in myself, that in all my acquaintance with him my hand has never met his, in casual greeting, without a loathing shudder. And yet, in the face of such an instinct, I would have married him! To what dreadful lengths are not women carried by reaction.

When the man fell, he struck the swinging drawer, and the papers it held are scattered about us. I take one up, and mechanically open and read it, heedless of the morality or delicacy of such an action.

"With this I hide my will," it runs, in the handwriting of a woman; "the will by which, unknown to him, I have defeated the murderous motives of my husband, Roberto Cantera. He does not dream I have already executed such a document. It was made in Mexico, months since, inspired by I know not what mysterious premonition. Well for me and my family that it was so, for I have been here for weeks a prisoner, my life attempted almost daily. I have almost starved myself, to avoid taking the poisons prepared for me; but now Roberto has sent to his sister in Jalapa for *palo de leche*, and in the water I drink, in the air I breathe, I shall receive that subtle poison. I pray that whosoever may find these notes will convey them to Don Gabriel Arriola, an attorney, Street of the Angel, Mexico, that he may restore my property to my sister and her children.

Concepción Tellez de Cantera."

And it is I who go in person to see the famous lawyer, while Josefita and her friends are taking the howling, foaming demoniac, that was Roberto Cantera, to the Asylum of San Hipólito.

City of Mexico, September, 1888.

Lyda H. Addis

The Haunted Engine

A Story of the Rail

Appeared in *The Argonaut* July 11, 1885

By such parties as were in the habit of frequenting the Transverse and Devious Railway Company's offices, Julius Wright must be well remembered. This observation is supposed to apply more particularly to the toilers and delvers, who were not likely to meet the man under other conditions. Socially considered, he was very much more of a swell than appeared at all justifiable by his position or his personal qualifications—always excepting that indefinable, mysterious quality known as "magnetism," which is, as novelists and telepathists inform us, quite independent of either beauty or merit. He was an insignificant little fellow, not over five feet four in his biggest-feeling moments. His face was alert and keen, but, to my eye, always fraught with the peculiar expression of a man liable at some time to go wrong. One does not follow any business for the years that I have done without learning to recognize the signs of potential guilt—that is to say, in faces of the active type. I never try to analyze a pretty face; I can not do it. I think no man living can.

Wright was a man of accomplishments. He could dance, and sing, and play prettily upon several instruments, and turn off little verses—*vers de société*—isn't that the term? And he was a manly little chap; could swim, and shoot, drive, ride, spar, and run with the best. So, as men liked him for his good-fellowship and women for his love-making and liberality, Wright was a popular man.

But I knew a thing or two about him. I was not surprised—not much—when, after a few days of uncertainty and suppressed rumors, it came out that Julius Wright had absconded with a sum of the railway company's funds reaching well up toward the hundreds of thousands—more than it appeared should have been accessible to him. The general inference, and the natural, was that he had betaken himself out of the country to the refuge of a government not on terms of extradition with the United States. Great, then, was the astonishment of the community when it transpired later that the escaped defaulter had been living for many weeks in easy reach of his pursuers, and actually in the employment of the company he had robbed. It was no wonder, said his late companions, with retroactive admiration, somewhat misplaced, that the officers of the law had failed to find, in the stoker of a freight train over the southwestern division, the spruce and fastidious individual who had been almost a social autocrat in the headquarters city of the company.

The newspapers got the story, of course, and gave it the usual send-off, with extra-heavy head-lines, and all the alliteration the dictionary would supply. I remember one of their phrases about "Engine No. 23 pulling into Walling with importance in every clank of the metal," and "the pluck and power displayed by the engineer, who had to report a notable occurrence on his run." Briefly stated, it appeared that No. 23 had come into Walling minus her fireman. The engineer's story was that some twenty miles back, as they crawled up a hard grade, the fireman had jumped from the train, discovering his identity to the engineer, together with a satirical message to the directors of the road.

" 'Tell 'em,' says he me—'from Julius Wright—that's me—their office was better than a school of polytechnics. Say, Stacy, can't I fire?' And with that he jumped, just as we started to run down the grade. I brought her in alone. I knew I could do it, and we was too short of hands to call one of the boys from the twists—the brakes; so I just came on and fired for myself. Tired? I should smile! and so shaky and starty I couldn't sleep—couldn't even set down and eat. You bet! The boy'll tell how all broke up I was. But I daresn't stop short off. No, sir! I just rustled round and cleaned the engine, and put her to bed myself. Well, I've hear men say they could run an engine sixty miles and fire for themselves, but I'm damned if I could! Twenty's enough for me," he said, with what struck me as rather defiant emphasis, and a keen under-browed look— for I got the story from his own lips, when I was sent out to Walling to work on the case.

I am not, as a rule, an imaginative man. "A patient, persistent plodder"—that is the characterization I once heard as made of me by our chief, who was given to alliteration in his rhetorical flourishes. Thus lacking imagination, it seemed to me little was to be gained by following Wright to Walling, whence he had gone with no form of taking leave. But to Walling the chief chose to dispatch me, after two of our best men had come back from a fruitless stay there.

"Certain uncommon avenues of receptiveness are abnormally alive to impression in you," he said; "I'd like you to go to Walling."

And to Walling I went, after some preliminary training under the fireman of a local train on one of the company's branch lines.

But the night before I started, I got a note that surprised me. It intimated that my services were required by Miss Mirabel Duane, and requested me to wait upon her at the earliest opportunity. Miss Duane had but just returned from a trip abroad. I could not conceive what she could want of me. Moreover, in view of my impending departure, it appeared not much worth while to obey her summons. And yet—and yet—her father was President of the T. and D. Railroad Company; Julius Wright had been a guest of the house, and I might obtain incidental data.

Miss Duane was a handsome girl, of the dark heroic type. I had seen her coming off the steamer, and I was genuinely shocked at the change in her in a fortnight. She was haggard and thin, as if she had been ill for months. She wasted no time in making her wishes known. She wished to employ me to trace up Julius Wright. Most women would have assigned some trumped-up reason, more or less un-plausible, to account for her interest in this man, who was virtually hardly more than her father's clerk. Miss Duane very properly assumed that her motive was no affair of mine. Her one concern was to spare no expense in finding Julius Wright.

"I am so very sure you will find a clue at Walling," she said; "I can not put that conviction from my mind. And when you find him, give him this from me."

I was obliged to tell her of my prior undertaking, and to

intimate that I feared the mission was opposed to hers. She tore open the note she had given me.

"Read."

"X Y Z thousand dollars" (the sum with which Wright had absconded) "were this day paid in your name to the T. and D. Railway Company. Your immediate return will cause the charges against you to be withdrawn."

"Here are the railroad company's receipts," she said, and displayed them, duly attested. "Now, you must see, the one thing is to find Mr. Wright. Every added day of his absence makes it harder to reinstate him——"

She paused, gasped, shuddered, and put out one hand toward me with a look of fright and pain. As I caught her cold slim fingers in answer to that appeal, she fell back swooning in her chair. Deathly as she looked, I could not bring myself to call for help. It seemed to me it would be an infamous thing to expose her to the indifferent curiosity and comment of domestics and chance guests. With my free hand I tossed the flowers from a vase close by, and dashed the water in her ghastly face.

"O God!" she moaned, "the fire! the merciless fire!"

Her left hand was clasping some ornament at her throat, dragging down the supporting chain until it threatened to strangle her. I bent to unclasp that clinging hand. It yielded its grasp stiffly, and the pendant locket swung into my own hand. The gold burned my flesh as if it were a coal. And with that contact an unaccountable thrill swept over me—a sensation like that we have when we seem to re-live in a dream some part of a former existence. Out of this vague mistiness of thought and feeling, I seemed to resolve the face of Julius Wright, distorted, full of horror and agony unspeakable. I started. Miss Duane was languidly opening her eyes.

"I fainted again, I suppose? No; pray call no one," she said, weakly, but with decision. "I am so grateful that you brought no one here—but you may give me, if you will, a cup of wine from the cabinet in the corner.

She sipped the restorative slowly, and graciously smiled at my clumsy speeches of sympathy.

"Then you will make additional efforts to give me relief, will you not? For this arises from pure anxiety and grief. I never swooned in my life until a fortnight ago. It seems contemptible to trade upon one's weakness, does it not? But—well—you men will let yourselves be moved by the sight of physical suffering, where the extreme of mental anguish would make no impression.

"Madam," I said, "what does that locket contain?"

She started with a haughty, questioning glance, that became lost in wonder.

"It holds—a miniature."

"Perhaps a lock of hair? Yes, I thought as much. Now, let me advise you. Take it from your neck, with care to touch only the chain, put it away in a safe, or drawer—where you will—out of reach of contact with you, and I guarantee you immunity from these swoons."

"What do you—what can you mean? What do you know?"

"I know no more than yourself—only that there is a subtle essence of relation between the material and the spiritual that our finite, faulty knowledge has not grasped. You wear the portrait and the hair of a person for whom you have a strong congenial affinity, and on physical contact with it your over-susceptible organization receives the force of his suffering—stay! It may not be bodily suffering—it may be grief, or apprehension—or remorse."

Her proud head dropped.

"I believe you are right," she said; "my folly has been so great that I have fancied I found actual consolation in touching the lock of hair I had arranged to meet my hand. And now I fancy that I can remember how every attack of this nature has been coincident with such a lapse of weakness. At all events, I will experiment on your advice. My very life is sapped by these swoons, from which I bring no definite recollection, but a sense of indescribable horror, and peril to Julius Wright."

All the restlessness and the intensity of Miss Duane's own spirit seemed to possess me when I went to Walling. And all futility and non-fruition of effort seemed to confront and mock me. It was easy enough to set any Walling tongue a-wagging about "the swell that fired for Stacy, and skipped between two days," but to the published facts no one could add a word. Wright had been a clever actor, and had given no clue. His record here was like the outward life of any man in his apparent station. Stacy was willing enough to repeat his story, but it was the same unvarying account he had already given me so often. His conclusion of its now began to be colored, as I have intimidated by a touch of resentment. He was evidently not a little vain of his unassisted management of his great machine in that memorable night-run, and jealous of hearing that others had surpassed the feat. Indeed, he had become so arrogant and unreasonable as to have offended most of "the boys at the yard." Walling being a division terminus, the little town was a general stopping place, whence the men were variously assigned to the trains dispatched night and day.

"All Stacy wants now is a Jew-stone diamond-pin to make a way-up conduc., but he'll have to sport a double chin before he can get to be a director. He'll be runnin' the whole thunderin' line pretty soon," said the railroad man, one of the group lounging on the boarding-house piazza.

"Well, he can start right now," said another, "and I'll copper on any train he starts. I'd sooner drive the devil's dump-cart than to fire on '23' again to-night. That engine's got the phthisis, and she's go'n t' bust and blow the whole crew over into Utah."

"Give us a rest," spoke up a boss from the machine shops; " '23' 's the best on the division. They's not a rivet sick about her."

"Oh, they ain't, ain't they? Well, what I want to know's what makes them sulphur fumes just settle down in the cab so thick you could make a sieve of 'em with a shotgun. I swear, I thought I'd choke last week."

"That's so," said a quiet little fellow, who was busily plucking out his mustache, hair by hair, "I fired on '23' week 'fore last, and I could hardly breathe; and worse 'n that, somehow I got scared, and—and—well, I don't know what was the matter, but I went to sleep—or fainted, or something—and when I come to, there I was lying full o' cold sweat, and Stacy shovelin' double coal right over my head."

"Them's me!" cried the malcontent.

"Scared! Why, my heart clim up and clawed at my tongue, and it felt as big and hard as a driving-wheel, and I keeled over. Gents, '23' 's freight, but she's got a passenger aboard. His name's Mr. Spook, and his profession's warnin's. He's served notice on me that '23' 's got a notion o' layin' down on her back, and makin' poached duck out o' me. I'll promenade over, and sort o' tell Mr. Train-dispatcher I'm caught out."

"Suppose he'd put me on in your place?" I said.

The men gathered about me with notes of admiration, both decisive and sincere. It was an off hour, and the bunch escorted me over to the office, and presented me to the train-dispatcher. There was much mock ceremony, conducted with a gravity that would not discredit Parliament, and much humor of a quaint, original cast. The train-master looked annoyed when he saw my credentials. Hitherto he had deemed me what I appeared—supernumerary "hand," awaiting assignment.

"Well, I don't like this," he said, having bidden me into his private office. "Couldn't you make your opportunity some other way? It's taking such chances for the train. Oh, you can fire? Oh, that's all right, then. Just so Stacy has help—I couldn't risk him alone."

"Drink?" I said casually.

"Not a drop. No, I guess it is the strain or the other night. He's getting all broke up."

At nine o'clock "23" stood coughing for her start; a great ten-wheeler, shining, mighty. The yard lights shone on the close brown cars of the through freight behind her, stretching back, a long line, like some articulated, sentient creature. A group of the boys stood near, and speeded us with good-natured chaff.

"Look out you don't lose your mate again, Stacy," cried one; "this is another new man, and it's just a month to-night since the other said "Good-bye, sweetheart!"

When I looked at Stacy after this, his face was as white as the aerated fluid in the tube of the water-gauge. We had scarcely left the lights of Walling behind, when I felt a singular sense of oppression. Our smoke seemed to settle down upon us, laden with sulphurous gas, as when confined in a tunnel. Our train was a "time fright" that ran but once a week, and at this period the line was clear for our passage over the whole division. Carrying the water supply in a tank-car, we had no need to stop on the whole run. We clattered past small way-stations, fast asleep already, dark, save for the signalman's lonely light. We clanked through defiles tremblingly, as if the dark mountains on either side were crouching monsters, gathering for the spring. We hurled ourselves upon the shadowy shapes of spectral bridges, with the indrawn breath of uncertainty with which man ever approaches the insubstantial and mysterious.

"Fire up!" cried the engineer; "he is not burnt!"

Since our first start he had been leaning on his rest, save when he mechanically tended the machine. But now he turned, with a swift whirl, caught the chain door-swing of the fire-box, swing it open with the stocker's accustomed swaying pull, peered into the fiery gap with searching gaze, and slammed the iron door as if upon a foe.

"Fire up! Why don't you put in coal?"

It wanted half the usual time, but I was constrained to obey. I had not yet wiped the blackened sweat from my brow, when he whirled about again and opened the furnace door.

"Plainer and plainer!" he cried; "put in more coal!"

He turned to the window again as I brought the scoop. The coal never was burned. I threw it over the side, impelled by prudential motives less than by a curious appearance that arrested me when I opened the fire-box door. And so, through the rest of the run, while the smoke gathered thicker, denser, and more fœtid, again and again, and a score of times again, we repeated that same formula—he commanding, I alternating actual obedience with simulated compliance.

The way-stations were thickening toward Belen, when the engineer approached me, after one of his wistful reluctant visits to the fire.

"You are a good lot," he said; "you have got sand. The others all fainted dead away—they couldn't stand it. Yes, you're a good pluck. Come!" he said, ingratiatingly, "you look, and see if he is there."

I opened the iron door. "Yes, he is there."

He caught the loaded scoop and thrust it into my hand.

"Throw it in on him!" he cried, "and burn him up. Perhaps you can do it."

I shoveled in the coal, then turned and took him by the arm.

"Why did you burn him up?" I said.

He cowered behind me, toward the tender, turning his face from the furnace, yet glancing back at it askant, as he had done all along, drawn toward it by reluctant fascination.

"Now, I will tell you," he said. "I know all along that he was Julius Wright. We lived behind his rooms, up yonder in the city—my wife and I—my Josie. Why—yes—he got me this berth! Do you suppose I'd have given him away to the company—not for ninety millions!—when he came out here and told me he was sweet on Miss Duane, and had robbed the company to get a start for her? No, sir! He carried that pile of notes with him day and night—you know how much of it I could have got by giving him up. He fired for me two months, ate with me, slept in my bed. The boys wondered to see me so thick with Sam Barnes, my fireman. Fire up! Is he—? Oh, it's no use!" He took up his recital: "He got a letter that night at Belen. There was a picture in it. See."

He took from his breast a letter and a photograph. Blood was on them both. The face in the picture was the face of a woman I had seen often enough in a luxurious little cottage on our northern bay—a merry, blonde face, with perfect teeth peeping through the parted lips—the type of woman who could smile into a man's eyes while she dishonored him.

"I happened to come behind him while he read. I saw the picture, and knew it. I knew the writing. She signed 'Your loving Josie' ! I stole away without his having heard me; and the first mile out of Belen I struck him down, and took my false wife's picture from him, and I burned him! But mark you I killed him first—he was dead when I thrust him into the fire-box. But I've been burning—through him—in the flames of hell! and burning alive! Fire up, and see—is he there? Oh, yes! I knew it. You see, on this run it is all reversed. He begins to grow into shape back near Walling, where his bones fell into ashes as I stirred them into the coals. The melted lumps of his jewelry are in my trunk at Walling—I would clean my engine that night, and I found them. Well, he grows and grows in the fire, until he stands like life on the spot where I killed him. You'll see soon—yonder ahead, where a pile of rock is over a Mexican grace."

And in truth, when the headlight flashed on an up-heaped cairn of stones, topped by a rough brown cross, once John Stacy cried in my ear, "Fire up!" and from the opened fire-box door appeared to issue something in human form, pallid and bleeding—the shape of Julius Wright. Farther and farther the dead man pressed the living, to the very edge of the tender's slippery step. Then I succeeded in stopping the train. The cab was empty, and a few rods farther back John Stacy lay beside the rails, stone dead.

San Francisco, July, 1885.

Yda H. Addis

———————
∽◉↶

An Unshrived Ghost

Friar Lorenzo's Midnight Adventure in the Calle de Olmedo

Appeared in *The Argonaut* June 27, 1892

In the City of Mexico, toward the close of the year 1731, Friar Lorenzo, of the Monastery of Los Suspiros de Jesus, was making his way homeward to that establishment in the chilly hours of very early morning. He had been keeping a vigil, imposed by the regulations of the order, that had taken him to a chapel in the Parish of Nuestra Señora de la Soledad, away out beyond the Zócalo, that lay about equidistant between his two terminals. A very old man was Friar Lorenzo, and his pace was far from rapid, so that he had been long on the way. By this time, he was so fatigued that his limbs almost refused longer to uphold the spare weight of his trembling, aged body. Yet he nerved himself to renewed effort as he heard the second hour boomed out from the big time-piece of the cathedral, at the very moment that he reached the entrance to the Calle de Olmedo; for the great fatigue he felt was yet exceeded and partly neutralized by more a potent impulse—the spurring thrills of terror.

Perhaps it were unfair to say that Friar Lorenzo was a coward; the kinder view were to consider that the sequestered conventual life had developed abnormally an extreme constitutional timidity. No priest in the monastery— nay, none in all the great City of Mexico—was better, kinder, or led a life more godly than of Friar Lorenzo. So meek was he, so holy in his life, that his superior ofttimes found it needful to rebuke him for excess of fasting and penance, and to exercise vigilance in the way of seeing that Friar Lorenzo took aliment enough to nourish his frail body, instead of setting apart his portion for bestowal upon the swarm of mendicants that daily haunted the steps of the monastery.

But in the active functions of his office—in aught that led him without the convent walls, to intercourse with his kind and encounter with the issues of worldly existence—to all such effort and contact the holy man was most reluctant, being ready to purchase exemption from such movement at any cost of penance.

The superior of the order had struggled long against this infirmity, and the mission on which he had to-night sent Friar Lorenzo was in the direct way of endeavor to correct the weakness. But alas! to-night the suffering of the friar was greater than ever—so great, indeed, as to be almost unbearable. The hour, the silence and gloom of the deserted streets, with their houses that appeared sealed and lifeless, and other lime forces, had wrought him up to a very panic of abject nervous dread—a fear of something, he knew not what. It was not long since all Mexico had been stirred to horror and dismay by the disappearance of the noble priest Juan de Nava, whose fate was not made clear till many long years after, and many grisly rumors were still rife concerning this matter. At that period, robbers abounded in Mexico, audacious and unpunished—robbers who would murder a man for the garments he wore. Stories, too, were related of men who killed for the ghastly delight of killing—whose crimes were inexplicable and seemingly causeless, like those murders committed in the dreary street of Don Juan Manuel, the stern motive of which transpired only long thereafter. Moreover, the ready superstitious credences of the day gave willing heed to the legends and tradition of the conquered Mexicans, and found in these supernatural causes for even vulgar crimes.

Therefore, it was no marvel that poor old Friar Lorenzo was full of terrors in his night-walk.

At the mouth of the Calle de Olmedo he halted; for its intensity of gloom and silence was even more terrible than the way he had just traversed. But this route meant a saving of many blocks of circuit, and after a brief hesitation, crossing himself and kissing his crucifix, which he firmly believed contained a splinter of the true cross, the old man entered the dark thoroughfare, murmuring, as he went, his prayers. He had scarcely passed the corner when he started so violently as to stagger and almost lose his footing, for his gown brushed and caused to rattle slightly the sword of a man standing silent and motionless in the embrasure of a doorway. Friar Lorenzo shuddered as he felt the eyes of the unknown bent piercingly upon him, and he quickened his steps to hurry onward. He had traversed half the block, and was beginning to breathe more freely, when he heard behind him the dull fall of footsteps following after—not in haste, but with the assured, deliberate measure that told of the pursuer's conviction that he could overtake this object of his pursuit without undue exertion. And, in truth, it was but a moment before the echo of that firm, determined tread sounded close beside the shuffling, uncertain feet of the friar, who commended himself to the infinite mercy of God, as he felt the presence of his pursuer. For some paces the two walked side by side in unbroken silence, and the monk was conscious of the sidelong, scrutinizing looks of the other.

Presently, "Delay thee, holy friar," spoke the object of his terror; "I have need of thy ministrations."

But Friar Lorenzo answered, trembling: "Spare me, I pray, your worship. I am old and feeble; since noon of yesterday I have kept vigil, and flesh and spirit alike are fainting. Your worship knows that to call at the wicket of any of the abounding monasteries will bring you succor, temporal or spiritual—aid far better than my poor, weak service. I pray you, señor, think no harm, bit I beg to decline the office."

The man at his side laughed shortly—a crisp, crude laugh, that made the monk feel as if he were shriveling up as he heard it.

"God's death! these friars are presumptuous! The ministers of God—the servants of heaven—so their creeds profess, yet they give themselves the airs of statesmen, and 'beg to decline' the offices of their profession! Have you forgotten your vows, sirrah? Have you forgotten to what service you are consecrated? Nay, then, I will have you—you and none other. See that you move on before me." He made as if to impel the monk by grasping his arm; but the touch of that hard hand so affected Friar Lorenzo that he reeled and would have fallen, had not the man released him.

"What—what would your worship have of me?" he stammered, faintly.

"You go to shrive a sinner," and, with that answer, his guide halted before a lofty mansion whose overhanging balconies shadowed the street. The somber cavalier pushed open the great zaguán, or entrance-door, without knocking, although, as Friar Lorenzo marked, there was a knocker of peculiar design, quite distinct from the conventional clenched hand, or lion's head—for this was a battle-axe, falling upon a buckler, and the two glimmered quite strangely clear in the gloom. The tunnel-like arch of the zaguán was all in densest darkness, save where a dim ray of light filter out from the crack of a door on the left hand, whither the way was led by the man who had captured the friar. This was the apartment usually assigned as a door-porter's lodge, in great houses, but here it seemed of dimensions more spacious than was common. The dark walls seemed to absorb, rather than reflect, the pale rays of the candle, yet enough of brilliance fell to flash gleams of keen color from the jewels of one who lay on a rough cot in a corner, draped over with a coverlet of rich brocade, glinting back the candle-light from the golden threads of it embroideries.

The stern man pointed to the outstretched figure: "Do thou confess her quickly."

The friar drew back with a start and a shiver when he had bent over the woman; for she was fast bound to the rude bed, made move-less by harsh cords that held her beautiful naked arms outstretched by her sides, and lashed her feet, too, closely. An observer of more worldly knowledge than Friar Lorenzo would have guessed that she had been borne hither from some scene of gala and rejoicing, for on her delicate wrists, and on her exquisite neck, and in the soft masses of her dark hair, blazed splendid jewels; and the zone of her corsage, showing above the coverlet, roughly wrapped around her, showed that the stuff of her garb was of exceeding richness.

"Wouldst thou confess, my daughter?" stammered Friar Lorenzo, drawn back to her, despite his fear, less by the sense of duty than by the appeal in her eyes, full of great despair and a mighty terror. He turned, when she made a sign of assent, toward his captor, in intimation of the privacy due to a confession, but that somber figure only laughed, albeit most harshly, and drew somewhat aside, toward the doorway. Then Friar Lorenzo, bending low above the woman, shaken between his fears and his pity, listened to her confession. But she had not yet finished, when the grim watcher strode forward, caught the friar by his lean, trembling arms, and cried, "Have done! thou art making pretext! Too long this wretched woman has lived already!" and, so against her wild entreaties, and the friar's protests, he dragged the minister away, and thrust him forth into the street.

The friar, half-stunned, yet half-desperate with the thoughts awakened by his foreboding, and the tale heard from the woman, called, prayed, and knocked, beating his frail hands on the heavy bronze-bossed portal in a very frenzy. But the massive wood gave back only the sound of his blows, and that but dully. At last, despairing, he hastened from the spot with so hurried and uncertain step that the few wayfarers who now began to appear in the street shrunk aside from him with more of awe than reverence, and murmured: "Oh! the poor padre! his many penances have made him mad."

Friar Lorenzo was half-distracted, most of all with doubts as to his divided duty. Did his priestly vows as to the inviolability of confession exact silence as to what had happened? Did the duties of humanity and justice demand that he give up to investigation and punishment the doer or would-be doer of what, he was convinced, was a foul crime? And so, seeking to temporize for guidance, he would fain tell his beads to temporize and calm his giddied senses. But his rosary swung not at his side! and a flash of thought reminded him that he had laid it upon the couch beside the doomed woman. That decided him. No fragment of the divine, thrice-sanctified true cross must be left to the unhallowed hands of that grisly, scoffing monster.

Thus Friar Lorenzo set off with eager though trembling speed for the Palace of Justice, that stood then, as it stands now, fronting on the great square Zócalo, or main plaza, and at right angles to the cathedral and sagrario. On the bridge spanning the canal before the palacio, he met a patrol just setting out on the last round before sunrise. The friar halted before them, and, with knotted tongue and parched, stammering lips, gasped forth his story. The officer of the patrol sped back to the guard-room to summon the alcalde, and a moment later the squad was rattling along at a swinging pace, the friar, whose exhaustion was evident, borne on the clasped hands of two stout soldiers. Following his directions, they paused at last before the wide zaguán of a house in the Calle de Olmedo. "It was here," the priest said, shivering.

The officer raised the brazed battle-axe of the knocker and clashed it against its buckler; but no challenging voice nor sound of shuffling, sandaled tread came back in answer. Again he knocked, more loudly, and no sound arose within but hallow echoes. Then the alcalde rapped with his sword, and summoned: "Open in the name of the king his justice!" and still no key rattled in the lock, no clink of bar or chain gave promise of ingress.

By this a crowd had gathered about the place—for the most part Indian hucksters, driving their heavy-laden donkeys into the city to market, or household servants thus early out of doors for the daily sweeping of the streets. One of these drew near from a house across the way—a woman of more than middle age, bearing the bundle of long, joint-less straws, tied up with a string that make the short, handle-less brooms of Mexico.

"Señores, your worships summon in vain," she said, with somewhat of wonder breaking through the composure of her bearing; "this house has long been vacant."

Friar Lorenzo turned in a sort of rage upon her, his meekness overborne by his distress of body and his soul's solicitude. "Wouldst say I lie, impious one? Shall a priest not know where he had heard confession? But it was here, I tell ye! Open! open! nor tarry for her prating, lest the crime done within our very hearing."

The woman's dark face flushed. She seemed a decent body, and her countenance was full of intelligence beyond the common, as she replied, with protest as positive as respectful:

"Nay, his reverence, she were, indeed, a bold and irreverent woman who would dispute the word of Friar Lorenzo—aye! I know his fame for holiness, as who does not among the humble ones of Mexico? But his reverence is less young than he once was, and these daybreak lights are uncertain, so that to mistake one house for another is easy. Humbly do I assure ye that never once has this door been opened in the fifty years that I have lived across there, and my mother, who was portress before me, has often said that never in her time had the house a tenant."

"But open! open!" Friar Lorenzo shouted. Then the officer, impressed in spite of himself by this strange excitement and insistence, bade his men take up a massive viga, or roof-beam of cedar, that lay where some workmen had be repairing an azotea, and, poising it among them, the patrolmen again and again dashed the heavy timber, in the guise of a battering-ram, against the door-leaves, whose heavy planks crashed loudly at the impact; then the bolts sprung open, and into the zaguán poured the gathered gazers. No sight or sound of life greeted the incursion. Once inside the zaguán, it was no hard matter to shatter the heavy antiquated padlock that held the door giving to the side room; that clumsy defense was, indeed, half-eaten away with rust and verdigris, and down from the corners of the door-head swung veritable curtains of venerable cobwebs, thick and velvety, like ancient tapestry. The door fell inward with a crash of rotten, honeycombed wood, and every soul there but one retreated a step or two from the unknown-ness before them. Only Friar Lorenzo pushed forward, with an eagerness that vanquished his decrepitude, and then, from the further corner, came his voice:

"Said I not so? And will ye doubt me longer, unbelievers? This was the place, indeed! They have taken away the hapless lady; ye must seek her, but the proof of the place I show ye! Here it is among a pile of rubbish, mine own dear rosary, made of olive-stones from Gethsemane," and he came forth, as the chief of the patrol caught a cresset from the hand of the huckster, and blew into a pungent blaze its slumbering bit of ocotl (Mexican pitch-pine or light wood), and went forward to rake curiously, with his short sword, among the shapeless heap that the friar had abandoned.

"This rubbish—why! lads! albricias! (A gift to the teller of good tidings.) Here is a wristlet, rings, a great breadth of brocade incrusted with gold and gems—a collect of major diamonds—aye! we have found a bonanza! and—what is this?" He clapped his hand upon a long mass, black as jet in the red light, and with one swift sweep held it aloft, as high as his head, whence it fell to the knees of him. Then he dropped it with a gasping cry of terror. " 'Tis hair! a woman's hair. And—gracious God! See that! the hair of a dead woman!" For, as he stirred that dense black veil from the coils and couchings where it had lain for unknown years, a smallish skull, long kept in position by its once crown of glory, rolled forward and touched his russet boot. And from the dread crumbling relics now arose a dire odor of mortality, whose warning of dissolution and decay sent the stout soldiers and their commander rushing, with one accord, away from the bones and the diamonds, hustling the peeping mob before them.

"Aye, Padre Friar Lorenzo!" called the alcalde; "now, what a blessed thing it is we have a holy man among us! Father, en el nombre de Jesus, Maria, y José" (in the name of Jesus, Mary, and Joseph), "purge and purify us of this vile contact!" And he would have knelt before Friar Lorenzo. But a sturdy artisan, who had just sent his great red copper kettle rolling across the dankly mossed stones of the court, as he dropped it in the effort to catch the sinking figure—this grimy Christian called out: "Stand back! give him the good God's air, ye doughty soldiers! Ah, no, it helps not! his eye is fixed, his face is ashen—his body grows dead weight. Aye, señores, see you not that this sainted Friar Lorenzo is dying, for never yet lived through the day a priest who confessed one already dead—and how many years think ye have lain yonder, whither he led us, or the mortal parts of the poor lady ye cried out that ye had found there?"

San Francisco, June, 1892.

Yda H. Addis

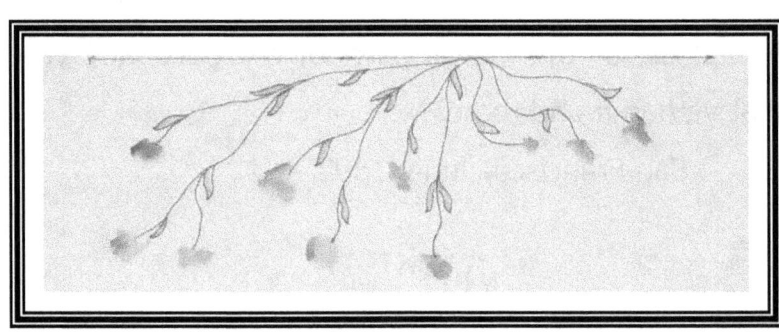

The Knotted Rope

Appeared in *The Argonaut*,
San Francisco, California, 1888.

Hacienda Amatla, México, 1888.

S eñor Álvarez is dying," with a troubled, even frightened face, José Cortina's worn voice passes through his trembling purple lips. Romero, the hacienda manager, can't quite hear the old overseer's words. "Speak up, José." Cortina takes a step nearer, "Si, el Señor Álvarez is dying."

A gust of cold wind swoops in at the door and around the feet of Romero. And with it, the high shrill sound like the shriek of a death agony wrenches at José Corina's heart, he sighs from knowing the irrefutable truth of this tremendous wind that blows straight down from the volcanoes, the icy wind that slices through human flesh to gnaw at the bones, always searching.... As José Cortina returns to the room of the dying man, we watch his figure move down the hall; we sit in a corner cowering together while the residuals of the wind's un-humanly-like presence sneak around us.

"Yes, lady and gentlemen," Romero turns his head towards those in the room, "It is customary, in the event of a death to invite all beneath the roof of the hacienda to take part in the last sacraments. We have candles for you; the priest is waiting."

Deep bellowing creeps up through the floor tiles, the hacienda walls shudder; it is the wind outside who demands to enter the sacramental rights of the dying. The wind so sharp, so keen, so entirely beyond the resistance of the thick adobe hacienda walls, it rattles the century old building like an earthquake; the candles go out, we are in blackness—caught in the impalpable finger of the wind while it twist through the rafters. We hear the birds cry as the wind throws them from their rafter nests. Clattering roof-tiles bring on the frightened howls of the bloodhounds confined in vacant rooms of the corridor near us. The atmosphere turns heavy and dank I can hardly breathe. I reach my hand for an earthy connection; my finger-tips touch the wall where I feel comfort from the unknown. But, there is a bump, a rough surface of an indentation, and then a smooth rounded figure on the wall. My fingers fumble the mysteries of the surface. What is this? It is not a normal adobe wall. Could it be? ... A carving? A stone carving? What does it look like? If there were a little glow of light, I could .... A dim light drifts towards us from the hall. As it nears, we see it is José Cortina carrying a lantern. We light out candles off the lantern.

In the new candle glow we look at each other: pleased on the one hand to see a known face, yet on the other hand, the proposition of attending the death of a man unknown to us is uncanny. Our guide, who knows this country, interposes: "To refuse to attend Extreme Unction would show ill will towards the dying and indifference to his soul's journey to his eternal rest. We must go."

I sigh and step forward, pause, and remembering the wall where my fingers rested in the darkness, I turn ... What I see knock the breath from my body. Romero hears my gasp, and twists around; he sees it too and says: "It is the picture writing of the Aztecs, pictographs craved into the walls. They speak of the wind that is here now with us, the wind that rolls down the volcanoes, a wind so entirely beyond the resistance of a man's endurance, that the clear-eyed Aztecs, quick like their descendants, to catch the salient characteristic of any matter, it is the wind's deadly force they show by that symbol of a human skeleton, pierced through the chest by an arrow."

We grope our way through the hallway until we reach the chamber of the dying man. At last we arrive breathless, at the little anteroom, a servant hands us lighted candles, and we steal into the bed-chamber where the centenarian lies dying.

He has been a powerful man, this Don Cipriano Álvarez, and even now he looks no feebler, no older, than many a man half his years. Around his bed are gathered the entire household, less those who now come in with us, and they and we take our places, kneeling, bearing the lighted candles.

"Do ye believe"—the priest looks around upon us as if convinced of our heresy—"in the Blessed Trinity: the Father, the Son and the Holy Ghost?"

And "We do believe," we answer. And so on through the Credo, and to the administration of the Communion.

When the priest bends over the sick man with the holy wafer, Don Cipriano Álvarez suddenly sits up in his bed, and pushes away the priest's hand.

"Get away with your bread and your wine!" he orders in a voice deep and resonant; "you have absolved me as one in the grasp of death and beyond confession, and in that I have fooled you. I held my tongue because I didn't want to answer. I don't believe in your religious hooey of repentance nor absolution. Why should I? I have the same feelings that made me do it then and those feelings are strong within me, and will burn in my heart past the doors of heaven or hell. When the revolution freed me from the old Spanish verdict of my crime you thought I lost my mind in the stupor of old age.

Now I ask you, look at this!" He throws open the top of his dressing gown, and we can see trailing across his dark, hairy chest that is still muscular and massive, a rope that is knotted around his neck.

At the sight, those in the room gasped. Old Romualdo said, "The noose, Ah! Dear God! He is still wearing the noose!" With tears in his dulled eyes, he mutters, "it was for this, then, that he no longer employed my services."

"Listen!" cried out Don Cipriano, "listen! Don't you hear Andronica's voice and the hoof-beats of her horse on the mountain Cubilete? Open the window so that I may hear it clearer. Open it I order, Open the window!

He is leaning forward towards the window, his swarthy face alight, impassioned. But the servants huddle together, frightened either at his macabre manner or at his blasphemy and no one moves to obey him. Then he tries to throw himself from the bed towards the window, but old Romualdo catches and holds him feebly, and cries to us, I beg you, open the window before he goes mad." The window is thrown open. At that moment the violent storm lulls and from some unknown silent stratum far away, echoing down the steep sides of Cubilete, everyone hears the thunder of a horse dashing along the rocky road, mixed with shrikes of a woman.

The centenarian raises himself again, and looks about with an air of triumph, as if the sound were sweet as music.

"Do you hear it? After all these years, it is the same. I do not free her. I am her master." As he speaks the words, he lifts his hands to the rope around his neck, as if it burned him, he gasps, shudders, and falls back on his pillows lifeless, as the priest makes the sign of the cross above him.

We watch by the body for the rest of the night, for the people of the hacienda are so much shocked and terrified at the closing scene of this dark life that they will not even hold the usual *duelo*. And from the priest and old Romualdo, crouched on the floor beside the bed of his master, we hear the dead man's story.

Part 2

Cipriano Soto Álvarez was a Spaniard, a Castilian, raised and educated in England, for the specific purpose of learning better business habits so that he might manage the affairs of the sugar plantations of Amatla. In those days, a decade before Mexico's independence from Spain, in those days Amatla was a Carmelites monastery, and the revenues of the hacienda were enormous. Friar Blas Álvarez, Cipriano's uncle, was the head of this brotherhood, and he, growing aged, was more than relieved to turn the management of the hacienda to his nephew. Young Álvarez was a man of passions as deep and intense as they were fiery, and the extent of his power at the monastery hacienda did not teach him self-denial. Of all the exterior matters, he was virtually master. True he lived within the monastery walls, and its discipline was rigorous. But his days spent out side and riding from one section to another across the broad domain, his comings and goings were irregular, and thus allowed the worldly benefits of the community.

It was on one of his wild rides about the country, on the business of the plantation, that he first saw Andronica Valles. Far up the mountain Cubilete, that was an outpost of the greater volcanoes, as it were, a stepping-stone to its vastness—far up, so far that it lay already among the pine trees, there nestled in a clay court hollow, a little hamlet, named, from the character of the soil there, El Barral, the place of clay, or clay-bank. Here lived a handful of simple people, who molded large pots and baked them in great earthen kilns, then sold them to the plantations. They were used to cook brown sugar into *piloncillos.* It was not a profitable business, for the pots sold for next to nothing, but it was a steady business because the demand was constant. So the simple villagers turned and baked the pots, then carried them down the steep mountain road into the valley, to Amatla, and other plantations. Andronica Valles lived at El Barral; she was the daughter a potter, and the day that Cipriano Álvarez saw her first she was descending the steep and rocky roadway, with half a dozen pots loaded upon her shoulders. She stepped painfully aside to the horseman pass her by, nor did she raise her glance to see him. But Cipriano Álvarez was struck by the suggestion of her willowy slight figure bent under its burden, all covered in the disguising coarse blue woolen skirt and huipil. He reined his horse beside her and with some imperative challenge as to her name, the place she lived and to where she was taking the pots.

"I am called Andronica Valles, most humble of your servants, sir," she said, using the accepted form of speech to the lord of the manor. "I am daughter to Toribio Valles We live at El Barral up yonder, and I am carrying the pots to Santa Lucia."

Dark with rich, soft brownness of her people, with her skin of velvet, her beauty was luscious and tempting as the sunlit downiness of a peach in a southern orchard. Here was no haughty type of an oppressed or captive Indian princess, but the quiet, timid, gentle air of womanhood that has been a temptation and a stimulant to hot-blooded man since the world began.

"You will not take the pots to Santa Lucia," said Cipriano Álvarez; "instead to Amatla—these and all you have in the future. And tell my steward to give you another three pesetas on the dozen, by my orders."

He put the spurs to his black horse, Santana, and rode

away down the mountain side, as if he was already ashamed or repented of the interest he had shown in a peon girl. Andronica labored onward. Heavy as were the burdens laid upon her, they had not yet deadened the supple grace of her young limbs, any more than labor and privation had affected the seductive sweetness of her countenance that might later become the leathery, un-human mask that comes with the even middle age to most women of her race and class.

When she went up the steep, cobble-stones incline, and in through the great vaulted gateway to the office in a dim dusk, high-arched corridor, it was with steps that flagged and wavered, not so much from fatigue as from misgiving. She had seldom come to Amatla with her pots. There had been something between her father and the steward—a question of a few cents that the poor Indian claimed that had not been paid for his wares, while the other raged at the accusation and had physically thrown Toribio Valles out of the plantation office. The Indian, all meek and humble as he was, had gone no more to Amatla, and Andronica also had passed by to the farther hacienda of Santa Lucia, except on the rare occasions when there was no need for the merchandise or when her over-worked physical forces failed her. But today the steward looked upon her with similes of honey, praised the excellence of the wares she brought him, and gave her the additional peseta of which Cipriano Álvarez had spoken.

But Andronica was ill at ease. She could perceive that all this attention and solicitude were something abnormal; and she was acutely conscious of the presence of the young man, swarthy and dark-bearded, sitting behind the tall desk by the window, who heard intently, she was sure, all that passed between her and the steward.

She turned the coins irresolutely in her hands when she received the money. "I don't know," she stammered, "this other money—it is too much—my father will be angry."

Cipriano looked up, and the steward scanned her curiously. Spaniards both, accustomed to the easy acceptation of pauperism in the old world, they could not understand how one of her humble position could hesitate to receive a gift of money, from whatever source it should come. At a look from his master, the steward spoke to her with words of reassurance, insinuation, of kindly import. But Andronica shook her head, and laid the money upon the desk before her.

"My father would be angry—and—and—I fear that Marcos would not approve."

A flash of distrust and jealousy leaped into the deep-set black eyes of Cipriano Álvarez. He glanced at the steward.

"And who may be this Marcos?" said the steward with condescension.

"Marcos—he is my *novio*," said the girl, a deep blush burning over her face; drawing her *huipil* about her, she leaped down the incline, and sped out upon the road like some wild creature, scarcely pausing even for reverence before a little squad of the monks that was entering.

The steward looked at Álvarez with a grin of malice. "For a *peona*, she is ungrateful. Better give her up, *mi amo*."

Cipriano muttered an oath into his black beard: "I will never give her up. So long as she lives—no, so long as I live, for I am to survive her—will I keep before me the thought of vengeance of the *peona* who has mocked me with her Marcos!"

From that day on, young Álvarez seemed to have but one object in life—the pursuit of Andronica Valles. Day by day his big black horse strained his steel-set sinews up the mountain road that led to El Barral. Another man would have fallen behind in the administration of his affairs, but not Cipriano Álvarez. Among the peasants who were his workmen, the power of his strange, wild temper was staggering. The work went on in the rustling cane-fields as diligently as ever, and half-naked panting workmen in the old vaulted crushing-rooms and vat-halls of the convent-mill dripped as wet with sweat while the administrator was scouring Cubilete as when he stood over them with a lash that was sharp and a tongue that was sharper.

Only with the people of El Barral was his power futile. There he was also feared, and most cordially hated; but as the people were not, strictly speaking, in peonage to Amatla, it was easier for them to shun him. Whenever he rode into the rocky street of the little hamlet, the little children, playing about the doorways, scattered and scuttled to their places of hiding, like frightened rabbits or partridges that hear the footsteps of the hunter. Their elders did not run away, but they stood about in sober, brooding silence, such as might chance at the moment to be idle, and gave to the intruder no greeting, except in reluctant response to his salutations, whereas they would greet him with imitation of enthusiasm at the approach of the outsider, and hail him with "God be with you!" He made trips to the cane-thatched hut of Toribio Valles; and having learned of Toribio Valles mis-adventures with the steward, he tried to soothe the Indian, and to lure him back to trade again with Amatla on offers of great advantage, in compensation, as he said, for the indignity from the steward.

But Toribio Valles would not be convinced. "Where the foot has once slipped," he declared grimly, "the ground will long remain dangerous, and betray one's step at any moment. I do not want to see the face of the man down yonder. The fathers of Amatla are kind and charitable to the Indians, but we do not deal with them directly."

Cipriano Álvarez winced at the imputation, which nevertheless did not turn him from his purpose. What had greater effect with him was the fact that Toribio Valles, on the occasion of his first visit, sent Andronica roundly about her business, speaking to her in some dialect unintelligible to the eager listener; and never thereafter did he more than catch a glimpse of her, flitting away into the forest as he neared the premises. While he sat under the poor roof of Toribio Valles, his was all the hospitality which was part of the creed of that simple people. But he could but perceive that this hospitality, if ungrudging, had not the spontaneous warmth and eagerness of attention that was customary. The knowledge brought him a certain discomfort, for he was only human; but no more than he might have felt if the cattle in the fields or the horses down yonder in the hacienda stalls had shown dumbly that his presence troubled and molested them. On the other hand, this passive resistance that he encountered only fanned the scathing flame of his passion and the sullen embers of his resolve.

Thus it befell that he rode up to El Barral, one sunny morning, meaning to settle the matter at once and forever to his satisfaction. The imperious egotism of his nature, strengthened by the habit of domination, had ill prepared the man to bear opposition, and he expected none from these humble people, taught an abject submission by the bitter experience of a long rule that was virtually slavery.

Cipriano Álvarez flung his horse's bridle to the *mozo*

riding behind him, and entered the poor hut of Toribio Valles.

"I have come here for your daughter," he said, without any preface.

The old man lifted his gaze from his potter's wheel whereon he was shaping a mass of clay into a form from a mould.

"Since when has my master been thinking," he said, "of marriage?"

Álvarez stared at him as if he had spoke some strange unintelligible gibberish, instead of very fair Spanish. That this man, this creature, might be possessed of a sense of humor never entered the head of a Spaniard. Neither did it occur to his arrogance that a human worm of the dust might be tactfully holding open to him, the aristocrat, the being of soul and intellect, a door of escape from a position unseemly and awkward.

"You do not understand," he answered bluntly: "I am not going to marry, so it is not as a servant I want her. She is a comely wench, and pleases my eye. I will take her down near the hacienda, and she shall want for nothing. When I send her back, she shall not come empty-handed. How soon can she be ready?"

The old potter stood up from his lathe eye to eye with Spaniard. Notwithstanding Toribio Valles' Spanish name, he was, if not of pure Indian blood, almost unmixed, and generations of servitude and degradation had not yet defaced his noble type of his ancestry.

"For twice a hundred years," he said, with impressive purpose, "we have been slaves to the Spaniards, and we have, too many of us, learned to kiss the hands that smite us, to wade in the filth of our masters, to imitate their vices, and to pander to them, to worship their false gods, even. Some few there are among us who keep to the old traditions. We live simply, miserably, toiling like beasts that we may live, but we live purely. Every day we watch the lights kindle yonder on the great white brow of Popocatépetl, the Smoking Mountain, and hope whispers sweetly to us that that day's dawn may herald the coming of Quetzalcóatl, the blue eyed god;nd his own coming, this time, not that of false pretenders, worshipers of gold and silver. But, for that our eyes may behold him clearly, for that our feet may follow to the kingdom where he will lead us, we must have led sober lives, and clean, and honest. Some among us have lost hope, and fallen, as I tell you. But some among us still are steadfast and enduring. Such of us do not sell ourselves, nor do we deliver our children up to the lustful arms of a spoiler."

He swung aside the rush-mat that served as the door between the two poor rooms of his dwelling.

"Andronica, come here."

The girl came into the room; she was shivering with

shame and anger, and Álvarez could but see that, however exaggerated might be the beliefs of the father, the daughter shared them fully. None knew better that he how doggedly the Indians cling to their ancient faith, and how persistently they practice their old rites, shrewdly cloaking the truth, for the most part, with a very fervor of apparent zeal and blind devotion to the faith of the conquerors.

"Will you, Sir, speak to the girl?" said Toribio Valles; "she's free as the *chupamirtos*—the hummingbirds down in the valley, free as the silk of the cotton tree when the pods burst open. If she will, she may go with you, Sir, to the life of ease and dishonor that you offer."

Cipriano Álvarez turned silently, sullenly to Andronica. For the life of him, he could not have spoken to her of the end to which he had destined her, braving as he must the indignant flashing light of those great green eyes, erstwhile so tender and timid, and the fine scorn that curved her gentle young lips.

She threw back her head, so little while ago bent under ignominious burdens, like a stag that sniffed a taint on the sweet air of morning.

"There is no longer the hope of tending the fire on the *teocallis*," she said, "and so the life I would best love is hopeless to me. But Quetzalcóatl comes— sooner, or later— and his kingdom will lack people, for our nation is degenerate and unworthy to enter in it. What, then, can I do better than to rear for him brave sons and honest daughters, that his new realm shall be populous. But shall you be their father? You!"—there was unmeasured disdain in her voice, as she looked at Álvarez. "No! Never! Me likes not the sort of man who covers his mouth with beard, to conceal the weakness of it. Now there is one from Guerrero—he is like me—of the *Yndios.*"

But her father, wiser than she in reading the hearts and the passions of men, laid his hand upon her lips. "You are a foolish babbler. You have dreamed up an ideal lover in the semblance of Quetzalcóatl. Sir, you have your answer. Leave us now, I pray for you." For the gathering rage in the face of the Spaniard was a thing to see and tremble.

For all answer, Álvarez raised his hand, that dark and strong right hand that had ere now thrown by the horns a charging bull in the meadows, and—oh! Eternal shame to him!—with one blow on the temple struck down the Indian, old and feeble. Stock still, where she stood, Andronica looked at him an instant, as if frozen with horror and incredulity of his impious cruelty. Then she sprung straight at the throat of Álvarez, rounding her hands before her lips as she came, to utter a strange, wild call that echoed weirdly through the pine-trees. In an instant, her fingers were clasping the Spaniard's throat like little bands of steel; her hot wide eyes flamed upon him.

Ashamed thought he was to struggle with a woman, as he had not been ashamed to strike down a weak and infirm man, he yet found himself in self-defense, compelled to strive with the hands that were choking him relentlessly. But the carrier of burdens had the power of her training and her free forest-life, and it might not have proved so easy a matter for the Spaniard to free himself, had his man not come to the rescue and helped to force Andronica aside. And when she would have returned to the attack, she swayed slightly with the impetus of the thrust the man had man had given her, and her feet touched her powerless father, who lay on the ground. All the tigress in her died out in an instant. Her face trembled into anguish, and she fell on her knees beside the injured Indian, as the two intruders leaped into their saddles. It was time they were away, for the hut was beginning to fill with stealthy footed shapes, which had hastened together there at the call of Andronica.

That night Toribio Valles lay in his hut, dying. The blow Álvarez had given him, and the general shock to his frail, ill-nourished body had been more than his strength could bear, and his life was a question of days only. His people were about him, for this had been a man of distinction among them. His natural ability, his strength of character and singleness of purpose, together with his knowledge of the Spanish language, among those who knew only their native dialect, had made him a natural leader.

He waved them all aside now, with the one word "Andronica." His daughter arose from her knees, and came to stand beside the reed mat that he lay upon.

"You must leave me, my own, my dearest daughter," he said, in the soft language of his people; "this is no place for you. You must go—at once— tonight, over yonder to the mountains of Guerrero, where, near the caverns of Cacalmanilpa, lives your aunt, the sister of your dead mother. Prepare yourself, my little one, for the journey."

"No, my father," said Andronica, "I cannot leave you. I will wait until you can travel with me."

"It will be many days before I am able to go with you," said Toribio Valles, disguising his moral strait from the child of his heart, "and you must not delay—that will be fatal. Do not protest. Have you forgotten the laws of our gods of obedience to parents? Then do not trouble me with objections."

Andronica ceased to demur, and shortly knelt before her father once again for his blessing before her departure. More than one of their people made ready to accompany her, but she refused their offers.

"It is better I go alone," she said, "that way I may readily escape the danger that threatens. They will not dream that I go alone—for are not women timid? It is here that they will come for me—would a daughter desert the sick-bed of her father?" she said, most bitterly.

"Stop, my child with vain complaints and expressions of grief," said Toribio Valles. "May the gods speed you upon the journey, and see that you not stop until you reach Cuernavaca—for it is from the interlopers mouth the name our people gave the city of Quauhnahhuac, for that it is near the beautiful hills. Go there to the *arbolario,* and the herbalist will send you on to the carvers. It may be the gods have called you there, for that is the land of the young man Donato.

So, with her father's knowledge of human nature lovingly brought into play to soften the pain of leaving, Andronica set forth on her journey. She must descend at least part of the way to the valley to skirt along the base of the mountains, and so she took her way down the steep, shelving sides of Cubilete that she had traversed so often with her burdens. She was but a short distance from her home, when her quick ear caught the sound of horses' hoofs ascending, and a moment later, from around the sharp bend in the road, there flashed upon her the unexpected light of a lantern help in the hand of a *mozo* on horseback who threw its light on the path before Cipriano Álvarez.

With a bound like the leap of a deer, she sprung upon a rock by the roadside; but too late—the men had seen her, and Álvarez, snarling like some wild beast, spurred Santanas forward.

"Where are you going, ingrate? What have you done, that you steal away like a thief in the night?"

Andronica was young—that is to say, she was hasty and impulsive. She was a woman, and that means that words of bitterness and taunts hung on her tongue like dew on the spears of the maguey plant.

"I have done no wrong," she answered, "save that of belonging to a race despised and down-trodden—the race you others regard only as chattels, to be beaten or played with as suits your convenience. And I am going—ah! Where you dare not follow! I am going to the strongholds of my people, in the mountains of Guerrero, to the great caverns, and where young Donato lives. Ay! But he is noble, *mi Yndito*! He is a man! He is one a woman might die—or live— for."

She was wild with the spirit of wrong, she was elated with triumph in the sense of escape and change, and she was sixty feet away from and above Cipriano Álvarez. But from a silver ring among the trappings of his splendid saddle hung a coil whose line was twice that long—a cunningly braided rope of black and white horse hair; and while she spoke, Álvarez unbound the leather points that held it, and as she ceased, it hissed through the air and settled down over her head, her neck and her shoulders, binding her arms to her waist, as bands of steel might have bound them. Then she was jerked roughly from her foothold, and pulled swiftly down the roadway, and then—oh! sweet heaven!—the black horse was spurred to madness, and went dashing down the steep sides of Cubilete, while the woman's shrieks rose on the night, loud and shrill at first, but all too soon becoming fainter and dying.

Meanwhile, farther up the mountain, near the hut where Toribio Valles lay dying, an owl hooted mournfully from the pine trees, and the Indian opened his heavy eyes, and murmured to his watchers the refrain that amounts to a prophecy among his people: "Canta el tecolote, el Yndio muere. The gods be with my daughter." Then the attenuated frame gave one great convulsive shudder, the stern, patient face grew ridged, and father and child were together.

$\mathcal{P}$art 3

$\mathcal{F}$riar Blas Álvarez wielded great influence in that part of the county, and the life of an Indian, more or less, was nothing as compared with a scandal in a monastery, yet even so the nephew of Friar Blas was tried for his monstrous crime and sentenced. But deference to the to the churchly influence modified the penalty, and Cipriano Álvarez was condemned to be hanged in his ninety-ninth year, wearing, meanwhile, about his neck a noosed rope, that all should recognize in him a condemned murderer.

Within the decade broke out the war of Mexican

Independence from Spain, and the times were sorely troubled. Later when the laws of Reform were enacted, the church had to yield up her broad domains, and to Cipriano Álvarez came, by heritage the great hacienda of Amatla, which had been held as individual estate by his uncle, Friar Blas. Other times bring other manners. Under the new rule and order of things the old story was forgotten, its scene lying as it did in a remote and then, before the era of railways, somewhat inaccessible region. So that when the time came for the execution of his sentence, the crime and the sentence of Álvarez were buried in records long reduced to ashes in one or another of the country's epochs of warfare, and its memory was buried in the hearts of a few of his oldest retainer who were unlikely to recall it, and Cipriano Álvarez died in his bed, at the ripe old age of a hundred years.

Epilogue

"But it seems but yesterday it happened," mutters old Romualdo, "and to think he has worn the rope that he might still remember! He must have loved the Indita truly, if fiercely. And he has never loved a woman since. Oh! The dull blows of her soft body on the rocks! And the thunder of the horse's hoof down Cubilete! And the wild, wild screams of Andronica, as he dragged her onward! Just as to-night you heard them—I who know, I tell you! Si, señores! For I was the *mozo* then to Don Cipriano Álvarez. God rest his soul!"

Yda H. Addis

Over The Cliff

The Message from the other World—

A Story of Durango

Appeared in *The Argonaut* September 13, 1883, and

Part 2, September 22, 1883

I may as well preface my story by saying that I am the least superstitious of persons, and have made enemies not a few by my contemptuous repudiation of Spiritualism and its propositions. The supernatural is absolutely without terrors for me—or rather, I admit nothing supernatural. Many a night I have watched, and more than once alone, in silent vigils beside the dead, feeling no awe of their peaceful slumber. I have no toleration, even, for belief in any manifestation or apparition not explicable purely on scientific and material grounds. But I do believe in many still occult correlations of mind with mind, and mind with matter, some of which apply in this story I relate, whose apparent mysticism may be found in the laws of association, acting on receptive ground of psychical disturbance and morbid recollection.

Philip Conway was going into Mexico, and I was well nigh frantic from grief and despair, all the more intense and agonizing that I had no right to give an utterance. I have heard folks sneer, "Oh, not much suffering in the woe that can quote poetry!" but I know no spontaneous outcry, whether worded or inarticulate, more pathetically natural or painfully true than the lines,

"I was tired of my sorrow; oh, so faint! For it was double

In the weight of its oppression that I could not speak."

And so we stood there, Philip and I, face to face, with misery in our hearts and commonplaces on our lips, each too loyal and too brave, thank God! to purchase a moment's poor happiness at the cost of faith and duty. Not that our passions were feebler or our pains fainter than the passions and pains of our fellows; nor that bliss was less tempting. Rather that we were strong enough to resist, and honest enough to let ourselves understand how each individual concession to temptation helps to undermine the whole system of morality— how every little wave of weakness ripples still with fatal force upon ever weakening barrier.

I might clasp his hand as frankly and fearlessly as a

man, and might bid him God speed heartily as a sister, but I could not dishonor the privilege of kinship in lifting my lips to his, nor veil my true intent with the ambiguity of "Come back safely to me."

I swung myself aside to hide my face from those keen, gray eyes. I forced a pitiful laugh, and I said, with a grin attempting at jesting:

"If you find some cowboy or some brigand too quick for you, Philip, come back in the spirit and haunt me. Let me know who is your murderer, and I will avenge you."

"I believe you would do it," he said. "I have never doubted your devotion nor your courage since that night we rode together through the Sangreado Cañon, expecting every step to show us Manuel and Núñez. Don't you suppose I knew why you would keep on my right? Don't you suppose I understood that if they shot me, you meant to catch my gun and brave a life for mine?"

Surely there was nothing love-like in this, nothing sentimental. Surely the fiercest jealousy could find nothing to reproach. So much as that he might have said to a vaquero or to a tramp who might have shared his danger. And yet I was vaguely comforted, and it seemed a shade less hard to let him go forth to danger, perhaps to death, with so cold a farewell. He understood now, I was sure, that principle alone sealed the lips of my heart.

"Well," he said, "I must be gone. Good-bye. And, remember, I will come back, alive if I may, dead if I must."

With my hand fast in his, I looked straight up into his eyes, that were to watch over my welfare no more. I scanned every feature, from the brave, broad brow to the earnest, tender lips that should never touch mine. Some one was singing near by, and the breeze brought to us the sad, slight words of a foolish little farewell song. For months I had heard the refrain sung and whistled about the streets, with the wearying iteration of a strain that catches the popular fancy, but I had never understood the meaning of the words before. I understood them now, as I said my farewell—the simplest and sweetest of all farewells, I think—"Good-bye! God bless you!"

I heard from him here and there along the way—a message wired as the train was leaving Tucson, a line from Paso del Norte, a crate of chirimoyas from Guaymas, a box of shells from Mazatlan, and a letter, sketching his schooner trip from Guaymas thither. Then I should hear no more for a month, when, if mules were stanch, and no revolution should hatch to convulse postal arrangements in the unhappy sister republic, I might have a word from the wanderer from the fine old plateau city of Durango. My fears were lulled by time and his safety over the more perilous portions of the route, so that one fine afternoon I was in the best of moods, in full swing in my great wicker rocker. Robert Morton had brought up to me a book which he thought "foamy, but very bright," and I was at its brightest and lightest chapter. I do not know what impelled me. I felt no ghostly chill nor tremor, not warning gloom nor spell. I simply turned my head, and saw Philip standing in the doorway, just as I saw him last. Tall, slender, not muscular, but sinewy; the pale, oval face full of intellect and nervous thought; the brilliant eyes that changed from flashing gray to melting blue; the delicate hands; the long, drooping, fair mustache, and grave lips. I sprang to my feet with one glad cry:

"Philip!"

I thought he stood there in the flesh. In his fortnight his plan might have changed, and a steamer from Mazatlan was due in San Francisco two days ago. But when I went toward him, he motioned me back, as he would not have done, even for dear honor's sake, had this indeed been he. And while I gazed, astonished, his surroundings changed. I did not look into the familiar hallway, and through its wire-gauze door, but on a scene of mountain grandeur, rough and wild. Mountains, rock-mailed and fringed with great pines, one mighty mass heaped upon another, until the very sky seemed shut out; and far, far up the awful springing vastness, a little faint line, that was trail, creeping, clinging there, span-wide, as high as the flight of an eagle. Philip lifted his hand, signaling toward that dizzy pathway.

"He beckons me! O God! he is dead, and his body lies there!"

His eyes met mine once more; with the same look of repressed wistfulness they held when they left me. And while I looked—my eyes never moving from that dear shape—the mountain fastness faded away, then slowly the figure faded, while I saw through the misty outline a carriage climbing the steep, sloping street without, and the background of brown hillside, with the tall masts of the electric light defined against the marvelously blue sky above.

I would not give way to my first impulse of credence. The mountain path I had seen I remembered well as the pass of Buenos Ayres, on the terrible mountain road between Durango and Mazatlan. It was years since I crossed there, but I could not mistake that dizzy route. I told myself that my vivid recollection of the spot, and my knowledge that Philip must pass over it, had conjured up the vision I had seen. I said to my alarm that he must already have reached Durango, since I had heard from him a fortnight ago, as leaving Mazatlan at once, and the trip would need but eleven days. I brought all my intensity of hope, all obstinacy, and all incredulous skepticism to bear upon the case; and every attempt to disbelieve but confirmed my conviction that Philip had met his death in the bosom of the Sierra Madre.

Then very speedily and very quietly I resolved upon my plan of action. I would go to Mazatlan, and, having learned there what I might, proceed to Durango, making search by the way for recent disaster over the trails. Such course might be hasty and ill-advised; I might find Philip at Durango, or even Mazatlan. Letters might have miscarried or delayed, might meet and pass me on the way. No matter, I would try to soothe suspense by movement.

Alice and Fred, when they returned—she from her art-lesson and he from his office—were furious when they heard my determination, and its cause. If insolence and insults could move me, I had been very speedily deterred. They spared no argument, good or bad, neither taunts nor jibes over my old skepticism.

"I shall go," I said, and made no other answer.

"Then you may beg your way," said Fred; "no money of mine takes a crack-brained woman racing into guerrilla-cursed Mexico, after a man legally forbidden as her husband—most certainly not her father nor her brother. If he were one of these, it might be a little less absurd to follow him on the strength of a dream, for a dream it must have been."

"I have not asked you for money, Fred."

Poverty is sore enough at best, but, ah me! Never so hard as when money might compass the comfort or the safety of our loved ones; and yet, a bold heart and a steady will may grapple with and vanquish that grim, gaunt specter-wolf, and, holding the grisly monster by the throat, step over its very body to conquer fate.

I sold some trinkets I had treasured—quaintly carven turquoises, some lustrous big pearls from the fisheries of the Southern Gulf, one matchless black pearl, unique among the rest, and some pieces of the wonderful, fairy-like, frost-like silver filigree that I had collected in days more prosperous; not much, all told, but enough to bear me to my destination, as I recalled the cost of Mexican travel. I passed again over the southern route that I knew so well. Bustling towns and drowsy stations, arid desert plains and blooming tropic vales— they were like bits remembered from the feverish dream, as I sped past and onward, absorbed by a great despair and deep resolve. And so I came once more to the big, bright port on the white, tropic sands, where the gentle surf was breaking on the fair shore, lazily, as befits the latitude, and where the cocoa-palms were rustling overhead, with a tone of soothing all their own.

Edward Knellton came to the Hotel Iturbide, in prompt response to my line of summons, as graceful and as gallant a figure as he had seemed to my childish fancy when I had known him here ten years and more agone. I spent few words in convincing him of my identity with the gypsy-like child of those other, happier days. The fate of Philip was all I cared to canvass.

"Indeed, I am almost as troubled as you are," said this man, who also had been his friend. "And yet it is unreasonable. He was to send me a courier who would make the trip ahead of Gomez's return train, but none as come."

"And Gomez's train returned—when?"

"The day after to-morrow; you know, of course, that Philip did not go across with the regular party? No? It happened so, however, his affairs here detained him some days after the arrieros started, and he arranged to have Gomez stay to guide him over, on special mules of faster speed than the pack animals."

"They left here, then,—Philip and Gomez—do you remember on what date?"

Edward Knellton, the methodical, referred to a note book:

"They left here on the third instant."

On the third!—and their swifter paced saddle mules would gain two days on the pack-train; Then they would have passed Buenos Ayres on the seventh; and on the afternoon of the seventh Philip had appeared in my doorway!

With a certain defiance of desperation, I told my story to Edward Knellton, expectant of anything in the way of skepticism and derision. To my surprise he received the account without incredulity.

"If you will accept my escort," he said, "we will go to Durango; Gomez's train returns in two days, and another starts out on the following morning. I have taken no vacation this season, and it is the dull time of year for incoming vessels, so we shall be able to go without inconvenience. I will go up to the meson on Saturday to engage passage; perhaps you will like to come along. You may pick up information; but—let it come to you inadvertently. Do not disclose our connection with Philip."

His advice was thoroughly correct. Our only hope lay in wary outwitting of the guilty, if guilty there were. There was no hope of aid from the law in that land; and if violence had been done, its scene lay in the wastes of the wild region, among a simple mountain people, of knowledge the most primitive.

On the afternoon of the second day, Mr. Knellton summoned me to the meson. "I have telegraphed to Balle at Durango, and he has seen nothing of Philip. Balle would have been his first objective point in that city. I am afraid your misgivings are but too well founded. Indeed, knowing the country as I do, I have feared the worst all along."

Even my distress could not ignore the picturesqueness of the scene at the Meson del Puerto. The train was not long in, and the great stone-paved patio, or interior court, was still half filled with pack-mules, jaded, dusty, but still patient, and waiting meekly while the muleteers disburdened them from the clumsy, cumbrous aparejos; a score of those unwieldy pack-saddles lay about, and the mules, relieved from them were filing gravely toward the inner corrals. The animal known as "la cocina," from its burden of kitchen utensils, still tarried where a camp-fire was blazing on the flags, beside the cook briskly trundling his spindle-shaped roller over the sodden corn which he was grinding for tortillas, on the brown metatl stone. The attendant mule had an air of ingenuous unconcern, whose assumption was absurdly human-like, no less that his satisfaction over the bits of uncooked maza that the cook now and then bestowed surreptitiously from the tray of dough.

"Where's the patron's, friend!" said Mr. Knellton to a man loaded with forage, who paused to grin good-naturedly at the little comedy.

"Gomez?" said the arriero, with the quaint circumflex of the lower orders, "oh, he's inside there, drinking a *tragito* of mescal, else you wouldn't see this mozo loafing around to watch the madre's larks, sir. We don't know what's got into Gomez this trip. *Que diantre* of temper! *Vaya!* He'd just as soon knock my teeth down my throat as not. Shall I tell him *su merced* wants to speak to him?"

"Yes—no," said Edward Knellton, as I touched his arm; "take life easy, friend, and don't disturb yourself. We've all the time there is, and this lady may like to buy a tortilla from the madre here. All the better for his pocket, if the patron's not in sight, eh?"

The muleteer went off chuckling and complacent at the haughty looking gringo's familiar good humor. The cook, always dubbed madre by virtue of his office, looked up, and scratched his head with the same brown hand that raked down the dough into the tray.

"He's not half wrong, that bribón Epifanio. I never saw a man changed like Gomez this last trip. I don't know what's the matter. Swears even while he smoked, sir, and kicks the mules, like a devil with the hiccoughs; if he wore boots instead of sandals, not a beast in the train would have whole ribs. Por Dios! And the boys used to like him so well. There wasn't another train-master on the road had as many friends."

"Perhaps his sweetheart has given him calabasas?" I said, as Edward Knellton and I said, as Edward Knellton and I exchanged meaning looks.

"But no, then; didn't she run out clear to Delgados to meet him, and he drinking like a rat there at the tiendajon, and wouldn't even take her up on his horse, and she had to walk back again? And she's a darling, too—la Cruz! Not a prettier girl in the port."

"Was he like this when he overtook you on the road over to Durango?" I hazarded. "Perhaps he'd quarreled with his companion?"

"But what overtook?—*ini que compañero!* The lady doesn't understand. You see, the patron stayed behind the last trip to guide over an American that couldn't get ready to start with the train; and the boss counted on catching us at Rio Chiquito. But he played him at the last minuet—that gringo *carajado*—saving your presence, and the boss followed on to the summit alone, and found we were too far ahead, and his mule went lame, and so he turned back and waited at Duraznitos until we picked him up on the way home."

We looked at each other aghast. Perhaps all along we had been cherishing a faint hope that our alarm was a panic ungrounded. But here at the very outset we met circumstantial evidence almost enough to hang a man in any country where the administration of justice was more than a farce.

We left the cook, and sought the owner of the train. He was in the cantina, whose wares he had been testing freely; a tall, muscular fellow, brown and thin, with a certain austere dignity, in spite of his shifty, snaky eye.

"Como estamos, Don Mateo?" said Edward Knellton, with an air of extreme cordiality and trust; "What's the good word with you? Always hearty, eh? And how's my friend who went across with you? A fine fellow that! I hope you didn't let him sunburn that handsome blonde face of his?"

The Mexican looked at my friend keenly—a furtive,

sidelong glance, withal. Then he took out a wallet, and began to roll a corn-shuck cigarette, before replying. It seemed to me his thin brown fingers quivered around the hoja.

"Oh, yes, sir. El güero got through all right—that is, to say, he changed his mind at Coyotes, and took the trail that branches off to Parras. Said he knew his way from there—had come up once from Parras to Durango that way."

"And you went on into Durango alone, eh?"

"Yes, sir. *Su merced* will excuse me now? I must see to my arrieros; I want them to have a good dinner, sir. A man of tender heart am I, Mateo Gomez."

But when Edward Knellton made known our want to take passage in to-morrow's train, he was complaisant and at leisure in a moment.

"Oh, yes; to be sure I go across this trip. Why not? Is it"—with a sudden fierce look of suspicious defiance—"that the señor consul, perchance, should have any reason to think I do not go?"

"Ni que razón," cried Edward Knellton, cheerily, in the vernacular. "Nothing of reason, then. I go over to escort this young lady to her family, living in Durango, and I want hombre galan y valiente at the head of our train. My fears spoke for me, you see. Will you take a glass of mescal with me, Don Mateo?"

And they passed into the cantina together.

$\mathcal{P}$art 2

$\mathcal{T}$he train passed out in the early light of dawn. Mateo Gomez and Atanasio, the mozo assigned for my special attendance, came around to the Hotel Iturbide, with Edward Knellton already mounted. My valise was slung upon a pack, an extra hole tacked up in the cinch, I was lifted into the saddle, and we filed away to cross the dreary, wide, white wastes of sands, before the midday sun should sting them to unbearable reflected heat, even at this season. Long before the day was full enough to fling the usual lovely amethystine tints over the far mountain ranges eastward, we overtook the pack-train, plodding along the sand in the crepuscular light, like wraiths of mules. We camped that first night at La Noria. Mr. Knellton came to me, in the corridor of the fonda in the sandy little town, set amid scattering limes and guavas, and infested with the most venomous and ferocious of mosquitoes; he brought me a tine glass of *anisado*.

"You must drink it," he said; "the strain begins from here. From now on we may meet horror at any turn in the road."

I drank the cordial; surely no other liqueur is at once so delicate and so powerful. Then Edward Knellton led me out for a turn in the sweet evening air.

"As we agreed before seeing Gomez, you will seem to know no Spanish," he said, "for thus you may gather information from many an inadvertent speech let fall before you. Then, at each village or rancho, one of us will manage to lab behind, and learn if Philip was with Gomez when he passed that point. The man will be sure to know if we make inquiry while in camp; but after he is gone, a peseta or two will loosen tongues in spite of him. In this way we will learn when he parted company with Philip."

Ah, me! After that, not one little raised mound or ridge near the roadside escaped our vigilant eyes and the investigation of the steel-tipped slender staff Mr. Knellton had brought with him. Those tropic lowlands were full of strange, rich beauty; now we rode for hours through cultivated land, where groves of broad-leafed bananas, rustling, stood in fruitful rank; then jungle-like forest growths succeeded, where bright-hued birds flew through the foliage with long tail-plumage and proud crests. Everywhere wonderful fairy orchards and grotesque fruit-parasites grew on the boughs of mighty trees, and true to their parasite nature, drained the life-blood from the beings that sustained them. Gay parrots screamed overhead or darted chattering in and out of the mud-built nests—colonies where hundreds of the gem-like birds lived and bred. Here and there a banyan tree stood, somewhat apart from its forest neighbors, a colonnaded bole, with the strength of many in unity. Ah, how fair a country! What a journey would that not have been had an errand less melancholy been ours!

But every flowery thicket had a horror of its own, in the thought of might be there hidden away from the recoiling, affrighted eye of man. It was a relief to come into the foothills and lower ranges, where, with increasing altitude, vegetation diminished inversely, and so left less scope for probable tragic secrets by the near roadside. When we had passed camp at the picturesque Rio de Roncador; and at festive Pueblo Nuevo, with its inevitable function; and had crossed the thirty-one fords of the one cañon river; and had climbed the abrupt hill of Piedra Gorda, below the little village of the name, and opposite the great spire-like rock, un-trodden ever by foot of man, which springs upward to the sky from the valley at the shoulder of the mountain—the which is so steep that the peasants, tilling their little patches of corn-fields on its sharp falling sides, do in very truth lash themselves to the intermingling chaparral, lest they lose foot-hold and be dashed to death on the river rocks below; after these stoppages were past and done, we knew the end of our pilgrimage must indeed be near.

"Within the next three days we must find a trace, unless Gomez has spoken truth, and Philip gone on to Parras."

"Never!" I cried. "He never would be so false to himself, so little considerate of our anxiety. Would he not have telegraphed, do you think, if he had changed his course?"

"But you must remember the time has been shorter than your apprehension has let it seem, and telegraph stations are not so plentiful in Mexico. Yes, he would pass through two of the larger towns whence he might wire to us—true. But the lines may be broken—one never knows what to expect in this unquiet country."

"But why then did Philip come back to me?"

"That does indeed baffle explanation."

We had ridden back down the hill from Piedra Gorda to the ford, after our simple camp dinner, merely to pass the dragging time, and to ask for tidings from the people at the river, as we did not fail to ask from every cowherd woman whom we passed by the way, and every half savage miner, wresting a poor gain from the ore he crushed with a primitive *arrastra*, dragged over the rocky floor mayhap by a mulch cow, or by the man himself and his mates at the lever beam.

Here at the ford of Piedra Gorda, it was very pretty and very peaceful. The rocky breast of the hill stood sheerly up out of the charco below—a deep, still pool, in which a few barrels were floating, flattened by refraction; and the same force queerly distorted the legs of some cows standing knee-deep in the farther shallows. A *jacal* had burned here that day—a poor affair, with-built, straw-thatched—and three or four peasants huddled about its still smoldering embers, glowing in the gathering darkness of nightfall. Edward Knellton went up to the group and signaled out the evident unfortunate owner. He handed a handful of small coin into the hand of the melancholy wretch—an independence it was to the creature's simple needs.

"I suppose you know Mateo Gomez, all you men; he who has pack-trains over these roads?"

"Sí, lo sé." So miserably ignorant were they, they did not even use the verb conocer.

"Y yo también."

"Sí, lo sabemos todos."

"Bueno. Then, did you see him when he passed here to Duraznitos the last time, alone, but for a güero with him, a fair-faced gringo?"

Every unshapely head signed negation; every vacant face spoke a helpless ignorance. The burnt-out cotter furtively slipped his money into the folds of his sash, as if fearing it might be demanded again in penalty for his incapacity. But one countenance, and that the stupidest and the stolid-est of all, took back a certain tension with the effort of thought.

"I did see him, yes," he said, slowly, in the simplest form of speech, and the most hopelessly incorrect of dialects; "Mateo and a gringo buen mozo—ah, white and tall, too; but not as tall as Gomez. And when he went up that hill, a little trunk dropped off his mule, big like this"—he held his hands apart at about the length of Philip's hand-bag. "It broke and it was open; and it was full of moneys—gold, maybe, for it was yellow. But I never saw gold moneys, I, so I can not tell."

"And then?"

"Ey? Then they picked it up and they went on. But I thought Gomez wanted that money. He looked"—the simple fellow put on a not inapt scowl of sinister cupidity.

"You heard?" I could say no more.

"I heard," said my true friend in need, as we labored up the steep grade.

"But I can not see why Gomez did not give out that his passenger had fallen over the precipice."

"But in that case search would be made, and the money be found missing."

"Ah, true!"

When we had come into the village that afternoon, I had noticed, mechanically, a little child whose appearance was most startling among those dusky faces. She was an albino of the purest type. Her eyes had been narrowed till they showed the merest line of light, and to-night I observed that they had unclosed as darkness came on, and shone full-orbed. With a certain listless curiosity, I called the little creature to me, to examine those pink pupils. Her confident, coquettish little ways proved her a favorite with the wayfarers camping here. In coming to me she stopped to lay a hand on Mateo Gomez's knee, as he sat smoking in the doorway.

"Bendita sea la niña!" cried her fond, proud mother, herself as brown as the wayside rocks, and well nigh idolatrous of this white mountain flower.

"She loves her big friend Mateo always best—no, Senovia?"

The master of our train bent over as if to kiss the child; then rose up suddenly, pushing her from him with a force that almost felled her, and flung himself out of the house. When the outburst of sympathy and indignation was over, Mr. Knellton drew the child toward him.

"Ah, I thought as much. Be calm," he said, in our own tongue; "do not betray yourself and see if you recognize this trinket. —You will let us give your little sunflower a little gift for memory?" he went on. "Perhaps she has presents, even from travelers, at times?"

"Oh, pues, si!" the gratified mother brindled. "For example, sir, not twenty days ago, came through here with Gomez—iha! *iaquel ingrato!* he shall never touch my child again, rough brute-beast that he is!—came through here a *forastero*, fairer even than yourself, sir, and he hung about my Senovia's neck that little double cannon. A little daughter of his own he had, said he, and fair in the hair, too."

I bent to press passionate kisses on the tiny opera-glasses of pearl and gold, for the bauble that lay on the breast of this wee Mexican maiden, had been hung there by my lost Philip, detached from his own watch-chain.

When we broke camp the next morning, we very gravely looked our last upon the low houses, cane-ceiled, for when the sweep of the road around the left-hand mountain should conceal from us their red-tiled roofs, we would have looked our last upon houses of this mode and upon sub-tropical vegetation; for now our road ran steeply and suddenly up, and we should encamp among the pines, fragrant and murmurous, and among the clouds—ah, yes! above them. We should see clouds floating, like foam of the air, far below our way.

"Ah, señor, you felt—well, not quite tranquil on the Espinazo del Diablo; how will it be with you on Buenos Ayres?" cried my mozo, Atanasio. For, indeed, my friend, Edward Knellton, dear to me as a brother might be, for his great sympathy and kindness in my distress, can not overcome his very natural alarm on these blindly giddy roads, precipitous till a single misstep were fatal.

"Is this pass really worse than 'The Devil's Backbone?'" he asked of me.

"I don't think myself at all a coward—I have more than once faced death without flinching—but I shall never recall without a shudder that zigzag, steep road, where one doubles round a hundred rods to advance five, and sees one's friend half a mile away by the road, but yet so close that one could drop a stone over the edge upon his head, in turning a corner on a path a yard wide, does not overhang three hundred feet straight down. How is this Buenos Ayres?"

"It is three-quarters of a mile or yard-wide road, curving around the breast of a mountain, with a bluff sheer up, close on one side, and miles almost straight down on the other. The path is worn nearly a foot deep by the unswerving feet of the mules, and where we must go down at the farther end, a slope of perhaps twenty *varas*, there is a veritable staircase of holes worn in the rock ledges, where the careful animals set their feet each precisely in the track of those before him."

"Animals sometimes go over, I suppose?"

"Yes. If the packs are not well adjusted, bearing too much towards the cliff, one touch against the projecting rock loses equilibrium, and the pannier overhanging the precipice overbalances the mule, and pulls him over. Where the descent is sheer all is lost, but in some part a slope arrests the fall, and the arrieros lower themselves down to save the *carga*."

"The animal...."— "Is always killed. No living body could survive such a fall. Hundreds of mules have been lost here."

None can conceive what it cost me to continue talking coolly of this spot, where my dear one lay—I was convinced—dead. I think Edward Knellton persisted upon the subject, thinking thus to dull the edge of my horror. Perhaps he was right.

I came in sight of the pass as calm as ever I had been in my rocking-chair at home. Atanasio turned in his saddle, and took of his hat with a courtesy that was almost solemn.

"Señores," he said, "behold la cuesta de los Buenos Ayres!"

There was a little plateau just before the pass opened, where the train was stopped, girths examined, the steadiness of packs tried, and the arrieros ranged in position—so many mules between each two. When we came, in the last of the line always, for safety in case of mishap, the men seemed to be making merry all at the expense of the master, Gomez.

"Wilt thou go across *ciego* this time, Mateo?" said jolly Pepe, the madre, not my friend of the meson, but another, fat and funny; for all the men of this train were of a flesh relay, save only the master, Gomez.

"Of a truth," said my gentle, serious mozo Atanasio, "it is not strange that Don Eduardo has the fear. Here is the patron, who goes the road these fifteen years, never giddy before, and the very last trip he must be blindfolded when he rides into Buenos Ayres. True, he took it off when he was half way over, said the boys who were in that train."

"Better tie your sash over your eyes now, *amo*," said Yldefonso, slyly; "we won't have room to come and say, 'How many fingers before you?' on the cuesta."

Mateo Gomez burst into a torrent of profanity, and the vilest language available in tongue rich soft-sounding black guard-isms, threatening dismissal to every man in this train, and to every tattler in the one lying off. The men looked at one another, disconcerted, and started up the mules with their peculiar sibilant whistle, their "*Hépa! Mula!*" and the usual brisk fusillade of clods and pebbles.

Gomez's rage was frightful to behold—his eyes blazed, foam stood on his lips, and his swarthy skin took on a sickly ashen pallor. He fell into line before me, and all the way around the pass I could see, on the back of his neck and the rims of his ears, that his color had not come back. Slowly, silently we wound around that perilous curve. Far ahead, one of the men broke into a song, that sounded wild and weird echoed from the cliffs, but none of his fellows took up the strain, and his voice wavered and fell after a bar or two. For myself, I was still almost to the degree of catalepsy, my senses dulled, my only thought a prayer that Edward Knellton might not grow giddy, and a breathless, awed expectation of something—I knew not what—that I was sure would befall ere we were out of Buenos Ayres.

We were well nigh through the pass. Edward Knellton's gray mule had stepped carefully, intelligently down the slope to the broader way open before us; Gomez was still in the path, but very near the slope, when the mozo Atanasio behind me called out, wildly: "*Por amor de Dios!* Go back, man! Go down! You will shove the lady over!"

I had been gazing out into the vacancy of space that stretched away and down, at the left of the road. I turned my head, and between my little black mule Contesa and the encroaching cliff stood Philip! Yes, it was Philip, one hand on my rein, and the other holding back from the stiff breeze his broad-leafed gray felt hat. I threw one hand out to rest on his shoulder. It passed through an intangible shape, and my foot, thrust out involuntarily, brushed the vines that here began to cling to the face of the rock.

Gomez glanced back.

"Dios mío! Jesus Cristo!"

The eloquent force of a prayer was in the words, below his breath as they sounded. Philip glided forward, and now stood between the mountain wall and Gomez's mule. The master of the train shrank aside, and lifted himself off the mule; he stood on the extreme verge of the precipice, just balanced there. The mule moved forward. Gomez put out his hand with a piteous gesture of appeal.

"But you are dead!" he cried. "Surely you must be

dead! I came from behind, on foot, and pushed you over. I heard your mule crash down, down, down, till the sound was lost! How could you be saved? But since you are saved, you will spare me. I have suffered—ay! Dios! Dios! Dios!"

He had receded an inch at a time—an inch? A hair's breadth at a time—as Philip advanced. When that tall shape, whose face was the grand, stern face of an accusing angel, put out his hand, Mateo Gomez reeled, and fell backward, down into empty air.

"He has caught on the shelf," Atanasio's soft voice said. "Señorita, could you put your mule forward? We must go down there."

My faithful little mule had stood as if that steady, unearthly hand held her bridle. She moved on at my command. Atanasio followed me down to the wider level, where the men were already rigging ropes for the descent. Santiago, strong and light, grave Joaquin, and the lad Yldefonso were lowered down the precipice. Angel and Andres, Chico and Refugio, Marcos and Atanasio and the cook, held the ropes.

Presently a call came up from below, far and faint:

"Son dos!—there are two here!"

Then I turned to the men:

"Put the rope on me. I must go down there. You will not?—then I vow by the Virgin, madre santísima, that I will throw myself over un-stayed."

Atanasio fell on his knees before Edward Knellton:

"Oh, say her nay. Command her, for you she will obey. She is mad! The dear niña is crazed by the horror of it!"

"No," said Edward Knellton, "she is right. She must go down, and I also. Do lower her after me."

The ledge, where the men were, tilted up to the sky at an angle, forming a shallow ravine, gutter-like, on the mountain wall, and the northern hollow, always in shade, was half full of snow.

My darling lay on that spotless pall, untouched by bird or beast. His brave, proud face was free from bruise or stain, except where on one temple, a blue mark showed how a merciful blow against a stone had given him instant release. His had been no torturing, lingering death, such as he might have suffered had he reached the shelf alive, abandoned to his fate.

The murderer Gomez had fallen with his legs dangling over the edge, and his face prone against his victim's feet.

LOS ANGELES, September, 1883.

Yda H. Addis

𝔗he 𝔖treet of the 𝔅ead
𝔐an

A Legend of Ancient Mexico

Appeared in *The Argonaut* August 20, 1887

El callejón Alzures in the City of Mexico, which lies behind the church of El Carmen, far from the main plaza, was, two centuries ago, inhabited by sober and prosperous people, languid, because they were comfortable; of the wealthy class, so numerous in New Spain, living quietly and decently in the peaceful monotony of their home, until roused to terror almost frenzied, by a visitation of ghastly and horrid nature.

The most pretentious house in the street was that built by one Tristan Alzures, for whom the thoroughfare was named; a man whose business energy and integrity had brought him great wealth, and whose charities and benevolence had earned him a reputation of almost saintly goodness. So much may be inferred from the fact that even in this world, where deeds of goodness are not often recognized, Don Tristan Alzures had been rewarded. Honors and distinctions lauded upon him; the ground whereon his home was built had been gifted to him, although wealthy as he was, by the municipality, in public recognition of his spirit of enterprise and generous deeds.

But neither fame nor merit can give immortality, and so Don Tristan died; but died in all the sweet fragrance of sanctity, mourned ostentatiously by guilds and associates, lamented selfishly by those to whom he had been a benefactor, and even regretted sincerely and disinterestedly by one—his son and successor, another Tristan.

The son succeeded to all his father's belongings, except his reputation; that is not hereditary, any more than ability or worth. And Tristan the younger was a different sort of person from his father; painted in neutral colors, it might be said. Yet under his quiet demeanor, and slow, almost dull speech, was a nature strong, fearless, and true, and a latent energy and force of great momentum. He was not an enthusiast, this son of the dead rich man, and he took life very quietly. For some weeks, even months, after his father's demise, his daily existence was an unvarying routine. He arose early, took a cold bath that is in Mexico up to the present day the surest remedy against rheumatism, pneumonia, typhus, and all the rapacious attendants on the dreadful miasmas arising from bad drainage. After the morning chocolate, young Alzures went to the great counting-house, and there passed the day with only a brief interval at the midday meal. He took no siesta, and his mourning garb prevented him from seeking social distractions, if he had felt so inclined: thus, returning home in the evening, as soon as he had ate, he went to bed.

Taken into consideration this methodical and secluded life, and add that young Alzures's servants felt for him a respect almost equivalent to awe, and far too intense to permit them to call his attention to gossip, and good reason appears why Tristan, in his solitary home, should not have heard or known of the direful rumors afloat in the barrio, and the all too practical effects resulting from it. His first knowledge of the existing condition of affairs came from his one intimate friend, Marcial Rasgón, a young man of about his own age, and, as might be inferred, a happy and vivacious character—almost the opposite in every respect of Tristan. In the great sala, furnished with richness, sumptuous, indeed, but stiff and somewhat forbidding, like all the rooms fitted after the constrained style of the times, Rasgón sat awaiting his friend one afternoon when Tristan reached the house.

"Oh man! I'm happy to see you!" cried the host, embracing his guest after the fashion of the land, and prolonging the warm-hearted *palmadita*, or pat upon the back, with which the greeting emphasized. And Tristan led the way to the dining-room where a great buffet was set in dreary splendor for one, and clapped his hands till half a score of servants came running to lay a place setting for young Rasgón.

But the visitor was ill at ease. He had been waiting long for Tristan, who had not come in till dusk; and, although inside the grated, unglazed windows, the wickets were closed in the massive wooden shutters, and the heavy damask curtains covered the windows, a glimpse of the outside world was had now and then, as a servant opened a door coming from the patio, and that glimpse showed a sky already purple-dark, and powdered thick with stars. No longer could Rasgón restrain his uneasiness. He rose, and picked up his wide brimmed hat.

"I will see you again on Sunday, Tristan."

Alzures looked over at his guest with wondering eyes. "Ay Dios! On Sunday then! And why are you leaving now? You've only been here a short quarter of an hour—and for the first time in weeks. You have not visited me since my father's funeral."

"Now, as to that," said Rasgón, holding up his head

with the frankness and the spirit of a man justified, "as to that, you must know I had to go just at that time to Vera Cruz on matters of importance, and I came back only a week ago."

"A week!" said Tristan in honest indignation, "a week! Weren't we supposed to be together every day, and all day long? No doubt I am dull company, unfit for cheerful companions, and unsightly, moreover, in this"—he touched his black mourning garb— "still one expects a little sympathy from one's friends."

"Now hear me, Tristan," said Marcial Rasgón, who was moved by the other's melancholy bitter tone; "You didn't know that is the case, can't you trust me? But all day long you are absorbed in your affairs, and at night—well, the fact is, at night I am afraid to come here."

"Afraid!" echoed Alzures, sorely perplexed. "Why, man, in all Mexico there is no safer street than this one. Now, if it were the street of Don Juan Manuel! There, I grant you should be afraid, where a person is mugged every night in the week, and twice on Sunday! But the criminals never have come here."

"Nor do I fear them," responded Rasgón, waxing sullen at what he deemed his friend's willful misapprehension. "You know I am no coward. I think I proved that well when our party was held up by bandits at the Llanos of Apam, and again in more than one gun fight. But it is permitted for the bravest of men to be afraid of a ghost."

"A ghost! My God! What ghost are you talking about? I have not heard of one."

And now it was Rasgón's turn to look amazed. "You're joking, Tristan! You are not a comedian. But, I forgot. You are near sighted—a myopic—yes, and at the time your get up in the morning, you would not be able to see anything."

"For weeks past, this area has been the theatre of a ghastly scene. Every night, soon after the call to vespers—that mournful bell that, summoning us to pray for the departed, reminds us that we too are mortal—at that hour, then, as if evoked by the prayers from a grave where he can not rest, a phantom appears—a spirit—what shall I say? Something frightful to behold, chilling the blood of all who see it. And from that hour till midnight that disembodied, dreadful specter traverses this street, and no one dares to meet it. Why, haven't you heard about it when you go to church?—But no! You only hear the mass, where requiems are sung for your father's soul. Here, not a fortnight since, our good curate of El Carmen came into this street with all the holy paraphernalia, to exorcise and to ban the Horror. But all his invocations were in vain. There is no doubt, he says, that some sin against the Holy Church in life has put this tortured soul beyond the reach of the church's offices, and he can tell his woe and put off his burden only through the medium of some fellow sinner, who shall dare challenge his distress. To such a one, the priest promises absolute indulgence, for the good work he shall do, both in relieving a soul in torment, and in bringing prosperity back to this barrio. Why, Tristan, my friend, every one who can move from here has gone, from the terror of the specter. There are palms tied on the window-bars of the houses, and you know that before, not a house was for rent on street."[1]

Muttering some expressions of surprise, but less emphatic than Rasgón thought the occasion demanded, young Alzures got his coat and hat, and offered to accompany his friend to his home. Upon returning, he walked slowly back and forth the length of the street. He had resolved to meet the Phantom, and to challenge the Horror. It was not that he was free from superstitious fears. The training of the times, subject to the dark and bloody rule of the Inquisition in Mexico, and the traditions of Aztec origin, were safe to nourish and inculcate such beliefs. But the watchword of life to Tristan Alzures was DUTY. He felt it his duty here to brave the unknown terror, and his decision was simply and promptly taken.

He was turning for the second time from the end of the street, when at its extreme limit he saw—what? A

---

[1] Palms leaves tied on the window bars indicated the home was for rent.

Something—shapeless form; and his flesh seemed to turn to living ice, his tongue stuck to the roof of his mouth, and he stood sinking, nerveless, as the Thing came straight toward him. It moved with a slow, noiseless glide, and as it came nearer, it took the semblance of a man, still, intangible as a cloud, though definite in form. It would have passed the young man, shrinking against the wall, but with one mighty, supreme effort, he put out his hand, and gasped:

"Stay! What and who are you?"

The specter paused on the instant. A close observer, calm of pulse and unafraid, would have said that its attitude bespoke something of wistfulness, of hesitancy, of pity. But it spoke no word, only drew a long, shuddering sigh, like the last breath of life.

Tristan gained courage as he waited, and again he invoked the apparition to utterance. "Speak! What is your burden? What crime committed in life entails upon you to unrest after death?" Still again he questioned, but he could get the Thing to answer other than a long, sobbing sigh.

But the third time, the specter spoke: "Unhappy, you who must suffer the penalty of another's sin! Would any other have dared to help me! It may be that this shall enter into my punishment. To compass my punishment, this you shall do tonight. Go to your home, and in your bedroom, four paces from your bed, at the left of the big window, lift up the floor tiles, and dig beneath. The box you shall find there, you shall take tomorrow to the archbishop. I will tell him in his dreams tonight that you are coming. And with this, you will free my soul from torment. May God be with you now, and comfort you in the sore affliction before you. Farewell! Farewell! Farewell!"

Then, silently as it had come, and swiftly, the shrouded figure faded away before the eyes of Tristan, who was left cold and rigid by the ominous weight of its words. The gist of its instructions could hardly leave a doubt in the mind of the young man that he had been speaking to the shade of his father. And what a dreadful crime and suffering, of ruin and disgrace perhaps, was foretold by the words he had just heard.

Dismayed and sorrowful, Tristan turned towards his home, and once within his own room—the same that his father had once occupied—he set himself resolutely to work to obey the command he had received. Indeed, and in good truth, when he had made in the spot indicated an excavation some four feet in depth, his pick struck hard metal, and he lifted out a small box, so heavily bound in iron that the wood barely showed through its interstices.

Early in the morning, after a sleepless night, Tristan left with the coffer to the residence of the archbishop.

"His Reverence has just been asking if a man with a

box had not come," said the door-porter in the great arched *zaguán*. And Tristan's heart grew faint, for against the evidence of his senses, he had hoped his vision might have proven a dream, and that the finding of the box was but a coincidence.

The Archbishop of that time was a saintly old man, the sincerity confirmed by his holy, charitable life. He listened to Tristan's story with infinite nostalgia, for the young man's grave, consistent character commanded all his esteem, while in his heart of hearts the ecclesiastic had never liked Alzures the elder.

"Leave the coffer with me," the old man said at last; "God knows what awful secret it holds within! And yet, my son, it may be that we worry over nothing. Perhaps this is no more serious than some forgotten bequest for charitable deeds, or provisions for saying additional masses for your father's soul. I will tell you soon."

When Tristan had left him alone, not all the Archbishop's efforts sufficed to open the box. On it was visible neither lock nor hinges, and in the ornate decoration of iron with which it was encased, there appeared no variation to determine an aperture. It was only when the Archbishop, fatigued and discouraged by the futility of his efforts, leaned upon it with a sigh, that some refractory spring was loosened by the pressure, and the corner slipped, grating back. That iron-bound case held another, lighter, box, and within the second receptacle was but papers. The first was a formidable-looking document, written on thick parchment-like paper, and heavily sealed with the Alzures seal. The inscription it bore was this: "TO HIM WHO SHALL BE ARCHBISHOP WHEN THIS IS FOUND." The cleric broke the seal.

"I am three times a hypocrite," the contents ran, written in the elegant, formal characters of the Spanish scribe, "not content with usurping among my brother sinners a reputation for goodness and honesty most undeserved, I die professing the utmost obedience and devotion to the church, the while I obtain her blessing and absolution by false pretense, feigning to have confessed devoutly all my sins, and claiming forgiveness for them. Let me tell here the truth: I follow this faithless course from fear and shame to meet the just disgrace of my fellow-citizens, whose esteem and favors I have so long enjoyed, rather than from apprehension that mother church might refuse to pardon my sin. This is the story of my evil doing: Fifteen years ago I found in danger of immediate destruction the business I had built up with laborious care and patient attention. Excessive, extra taxes had just been imposed upon commerce; family demands were making heavy encroachments on my resources, and two successive ships, dispatched with goods for me from Spain, had gone down at sea, or fallen prey to pirates. I had no friends or family from whom I could bring myself to ask assistance, and I was sunk in despair. At the very climax of my tribulation, when all seemed hopelessly dark, and another week should bring full ruin on me, in the falling due of a tremendous debt I had no means to pay -- at this moment of stress came to Mexico City, at once for pleasure and business, my old-time friend, Fernando Gómez, of Guanajuato. The yield of his mines had brought him fabulous wealth, and I might have asked him for help to tide over the disaster threatening me. But Gómez was a cautious man, a miser almost, and I believe that at the first hint of my distress he would have turned his back upon me. I gave him hospitality in my house, and all was well between us. Gómez had brought gold with him from Guanajuato, and letters of credit. He duly cashed them all, and brought the treasure home to my house, and hid it in the traveling chest he had brought. `We are two rich men together,' he said to me often, `each so rich that neither need fear the other will rob him.' Perhaps that speech awoke the devil in my heart. Gómez had been with me three days; his money was all collected, and on the next day he would begin to pay it out for certain investments. I formed a black resolve to murder Gómez, and all the conditions were in my favor. He had a tryst that night that he wished to conceal, for he passed in the world for a sort of second St. Anthony.

"His tryst was for three nights in succession, during the absence of certain parties from Mexico City, and his plan was to go out early in the evening, and return to my house at an advanced hour, by means of a secret side-door, unknown to the servants, using the same means of egress to go out about his business during the day. Therefore he mentioned before the servants that he was going to Texcoco for a few days, and at night I ushered him to the door with all the ceremony of the occasion, in view of three or four of my people. At four o'clock in the morning he scratched at the side door, where I awaited him, and half an hour later he was sleeping soundly. All was silent. The servants were at rest in their own quarters, and my wife and child were at the hacienda. I took a dagger of finest temper, and, bending over Gómez I buried it in his heart. I carried his body to the room—itself a secret chamber—where I opened the secret door, and then returned to the scene of my crime, and spent the remaining hours before my usual time of arising in removing the any traces of my crime, and in transferring Gómez' money to my own strong box. The following night I buried the body under the floor of the room where it was hidden. I paid my debts and established my business once more on a substantial basis. Gómez' disappearance attracted little notice -- these things are not so uncommon here among us. I myself went before the Mayor of the City to ask an investigation, but what could the Mayer do? I and my servants testified he had left us to go to Texcoco. At Texcoco he had never arrived. It was easy to conclude that his boatmen killed him for his jewels, throwing his body into the wide lagoon? As for his family in Guanajuato, perhaps his heirs were content not to find him. From that day on I prospered, as all the city knows. But, although I die with falsehood and cowardice adding to the burden of sin already resting on my soul, I can but make provision for the ultimate disclosing of the truth, that atonement and restitution may be made. As I die a traitor to my church, perhaps that church's benediction will give no rest to my soul, and I leave herein a gateway of escape from the torments of hell, praying that my earthly fellows who judge me, that they spare insomuch my dear son Tristan, who of all this he knows nothing, and is blameless; and who is moreover, of another fiber than mine.

—TRISTAN ALZURES THE FATHER."

The good Archbishop read this with horror and dismay. There mingled in his mind a shocked distress for the fate of Gómez of Guanajuato, cut off from life and repentance in the midst of his sins; mixed censure and compassion for the dead murderer; and, stronger than all beside, a tender, yearning pity for young Tristan, the guiltless son of so deeply criminal father.

"And Tristan the son is good and noble," thought the

Archbishop; "he is honest, true, and very charitable. In his hands this ill-gotten wealth will do nothing but good. Wherefore disgrace the lad and shame his father's memory, being the case now that nothing good can result from so doing? Instead will I confer with Tristancito, for the disinterment of Gómez, whose bones should lie in consecrated ground. With this, Tristan will give generously from his wealth for masses for the dead—all hapless both—and a liberal portion monthly to the poor. Since the will of the dead has brought this to my knowledge, surely it is fitting that I arbitrate upon it."

But, even while the good old cleric, full of charity for the sins of his kind, full of love and mercy for the sinful dead, and great with compassion to the living sufferers—while, then, the good Archbishop pondered how best to spare the living with never a wrong to the dead—there came at his door a loud, imperious knocking, and it opened to the guards of the Inquisitor-General of Mexico, to whom the door porter had hastened to babble of his master's dream, and its strange complementary sequel.

"His worship demands the coffer and its contents," said the grim official in command.

There was nothing to be said. The good Archbishop, beloved through he was of the people—indeed, not improbably because of the affection commanded by his gentle and upright character—found small favor with the Tribunal of the Inquisition. To that court was carried the appeal of the dead Tristan Alzures, and the verdict passed upon the matter may be judged by the occurrences of the following day.

Early in the forenoon a band of workmen entered the Callejón de Alzures, and, halting in front of the house for whose master the street was named, they proceeded to erect before it's a great gallows-tree, in such manner that the horrid fruit it should bear would hang in front of the open door. Then came a group of the peons employed about the graveyard; they bore a corpse, the which, it was plain to see, had just been disinterred; and, with brutal roughness and ignominious words, they suspended it from the gallows. The while a robust monk, barefoot and clad in frock of coarsest sackcloth, stood before the house, and related, in sonorous tones, the details of Alzures' crime. It goes without saying that the rabble gathered about, along with some high-ranking individuals. All confessed to sensations of horror and distress incommensurate with the feeling, intense though it might be, inspired by the facts as made known. None could explain the strange and powerful oppression until, as the body swayed and turned in the wind, some one caught sight of a silver crucifix that hung form the straining neck, and then the cry went up from all that great assemblage: "The Ghost! The phantom that has haunted the street! The ghost was

Alzures!" Soon the great zaguán of the Alzures' mansion opened and from it a funeral procession, rich with all the pomp and display of a church burial, accompanied by a priest and layman. It moved in slow procession to the Cathedral, whereby, after imposing ceremonies, to the graveyard; and there was buried the mortal parts of Gómez of Guanajuato, exhumed in the secret chamber of the Alzures mansion, in accordance with the slayer's directions.

The ancient chronicles avow that the bodies of both Alzures and Gómez, notwithstanding the long period of the latter's burial, were fresh and well-preserved as the newly dead. The body of Alzures hung for twenty-four hours upon the gallows, and was then buried at the stake at the Quemadero, or place of execution by fire, where is at present the lovely Alameda.

Tristan Alzures the younger entered the priesthood, and, it may be known without saying, the immense estates of his inheritance were confiscated by the Inquisition. The street of the Alzures was renamed "The Street of the Dead Man," and to this day it is called the El Callejón del Muerto.

CITY OF MEXICO, July, 1887.

Yda H. Addis

La Pila del Corazón

The Curious Legend of *The Fountain of the Sacred Heart*.
Appeared in *The Argonaut* June 18, 1887.

I am a nervous person, in the sense of being bothered by noise—irritable, perhaps, would rather be the word—and a boisterous child caused me to move from the place I called home. I relinquished my once quiet room on the inner court, where my belongings were so accustomed all that they seemed to fall into their places mechanically, at the slightest touch of the hand. But he who works with his brain must care for his tool.

I moved to the Hotel Alexander, across the city almost from my former residence that was located on the street of El Sagrado Corazón de Jesús—the Sacred Heart of Jesus. Many of the streets in Mexico City are named like that—for some old church or convent which formerly stood in the street—aye, which still stands, though now converted to state or secular use. The Church of El Sagrado Corazón has not been so converted. Its parish was a very wealthy one, and it saved the church, by buying in, from confiscation. This temple is today the richest in the city, and the only one with the right to ring its bells for longer than three minutes at a time. But the gardens that used to skirt the sacred edifice have long been parceled out into city lots, now built over with many houses, and the convent buildings are divided off, and used as private homes, as shops, as apartment houses, or what you will, except for only their old time churchly uses.

For long after the Reform Laws went into operation, the Church of El Sagrado Corazón de Jesús faced on to a little place or square in which a fountain flowed. This square was once the main interior court of the church possessions, and it was only some five years ago that an investigative spirit discovered that the bit of ground still rested under the church's title. Fired with indignant zeal, he reported the matter to the authorities, the little plaza was pounced upon, and sold to the enterprising individual in question, who at once proceeded to build thereupon this large Hotel Alexander, in which, owing to the good fortune of its owner in finding a central site not closed around by other buildings, "all the back rooms are front rooms," as an admiring American journalist put the phrase.

As I have said, the hotel is bounded by the streets of El Sagrado Corazón—La Calle del Sagrado Corazón goes past the front; on the right, and between the hotel and the church, the Estampa del Sagrado Corazón; in the rear, Callejón del Sagrado Corazón; and on the left, the plaza of the same name, in which the fountain stands, it having been situated at one side of the original square, so that it now stands in a sort of open, alcove-like court, an offset from the side street which joins it to the main thoroughfare in front. This Pila or fountain supplies water for domestic use to a large section of the city hereabouts, and at certain hours of the day the aguadores come to fill their picturesque, three-handled chochocoles. Wearing their leather harnesses, studded and clamped with brass, their heads covered with straw caps sewed with leather, the quaint earthen vessels strapped from their foreheads by broad leather bands, in the stolid wooden faces, and rapid, machine-like movements, the aguadores appear almost like machines; and yet there is probably no other type in the city nearly so picturesque as theirs. It is a favorite resource with me to watch them daily, as they gather around the circular wall of the fountain, dipping up the water while they gossip. The aguador, reticent as he is with the rest of the world, is genial and communicative with his own class. I have no doubt they criticize most freely the slender shanks of young Ponce de Leon, at whose hands their chief has just pocketed a good sized tip for the transmission of a letter to Blanca de Nieves. Four of this fraternity are the Mercurys of surreptitious or clandestine love-making, thanks to the aguador's faculty of easy contact with the fair ladies, who may find difficulties, no less than the mistresses they serve, in coming forth to a position accessible to letters.

Accustomed, then, to this daily marshalling of the clan about the Pila beneath my window, their absence was the first thing that struck me, as I threw the curtains open one morning when I had arrived on the early train from a trip into Morelos. Nor did the water-carriers make their appearance, as usual, some hours later, at the time when they supply the kitchens with water for preparation of the noon day breakfast. It was not for lack of water in the Pila—it was overflowing its brink.

"What has become of all the aguadores?" I asked the man who performs the offices of housemaid for our corridor.

Ciriaco shrugged his shoulders. "Quien sabe, señorita; it is the day they do not come." Nor could all my insistence elicit further information.

They were back again the following day, however, much to my relief, for I had feared the walk-out might be permanent. And the next morning, taking up my *Diario*, which is usually the most prompt of the daily journals to chronicle current news, I chanced to note among its *gacetilla* a paragraph, of which the translation runs as follows:

"The day before yesterday marked the date on which,

once every month, the water in the Pila del Sagrado Corazón de Jesús becomes undrinkable for twenty-four hours, whether filtered or not. What can be the cause of this peculiar periodical manifestation?"

The languid tone of curiosity made me smile. I could but compare this with the energy of American journalism, realizing how, in the event of such a phenomenon among ourselves, the ground would have been thronged with rival reporters of the local and general press; how they would have camped upon the spot, tasting the water every third second, and causing it to be analyzed almost as often, and tracing the stream back to its fountain-head, rather than that the mystery should escape them. I set inquiry on foot, myself, in an access of the reportorial instinct, realizing the importance of the efforts all the while; I am free to confess my discernment was admirable sustained, the officials to whom I applied manifesting only a lukewarm interest, palpably prompted by a sense of gallantry, or else the more honest phase of avowed indifference.

"It has been so for many years," those of the latter contingent would aver; "the effect is the same, whatever may be the cause. It is only one day in a month, and that can be endured. Indeed, it is even the better for the aguadores, since the farther they carry the water, the larger will be their fee."

Vexed and disillusioned by this want of interest in the official powers, I directed myself next to the aguadores. Distrust of my race and my sex made the fraternity even more than usually non-committal. Then applying my favorite theory of the unfailing victory of the cultivated mind over the untrained, I told the *maestros*—for they will suffer themselves to be addressed only thus as "Master"—that it was my firm conviction the taint in the fountain resulted from its uncleanly condition. At this, the group I addressed, unlimbered their tongues no little, volubly assuring me that the reservoir was cleaned out every week; and in effect, some three days later, I saw a little army of them invade the plaza, plug up the channel with a bit of wood, and then, climbing into the great tub-like basin, scrub it out briskly and completely with brushes of zacaton-root. This process was repeated twice during the month.

Strangely enough, neither the fact of the water's periodical unsavory disposition, nor the obstacles I encountered in seeking an explanation of the occurrence, inspired in me repulsion or distaste for the fountain itself. On the contrary, I grew really fond of the rough, inartistic stone structure, set like an enormous muffin-ring at the side of the bare and treeless plaza. Especially at night did it seem less harsh and unattractive; then were hushed the strident voices of the parrots that all day long squawked on their respective perches, one at each of the three little pottery shops behind the hotel; then no longer could I hear the un-tuned piano hammered all day long across the way. The grim, dingy facades of the houses around the narrow plaza were softened in the darkness, and an old-fashioned lantern, swung from a wire extended from one of my balconies to another opposite, cast a light that wavered and shifted with a certain romantic quality, as the lamp swayed in the wind. It gave a sense of companionship in the lonely nights when I was wakeful, to listen to the plash of the water, pouring into the basin below, and often I would arise and sit in the balcony, that I might hear it more plainly. I had been extremely busy for some days, and had lost the run of time, when I awakened one night, softly, without a start, and with a curious, impersonal sense of interest in something—I knew not what. I arose and wrapped myself warmly, and went into the balcony of my little sitting-room, giving on the back street at right angles to the side toward the plaza, and overlooking, would one but lean over the balustrade, the entrance to the church of El Sagrado Corazón. Leaning and looking, still with that indefinite and tranquil expectation, I saw two figures emerge form the gateway of the temple, and move along the street toward me. I smiled. "Some young woman with an over-complaisant *dueña* has come to keep a tryst at the church, and has found the lover recreant." I concluded this because there was somewhat of despondency and heaviness in their movement. Then it occurred to me that they might have come to invoke the offices of the church in behalf of the sick or dying. They came nearer, and passed beneath my window, and then I saw that instead of the matronly protector, the taller shape was the figure of a priest in his long cassock.

What happened next became the strangest chapter of my life. I could swear on my death-bed that no sound broke the calm silence of the night, save the falling of the water in the fountain, and the insistent warbles of a mocking-bird near by, that would sing all night long when there was moonlight, its voice sounding weird and unnatural at such unwonted hours. Yet, notwithstanding, I know—I know—that I heard every word spoken by that strange pair as if their thoughts had echoed in my brain. It was as if I were the vehicle for the formulating of the unuttered thought of incorporate brains—as if some subtle medium of communication conveyed to me what they said.

"I beg, no I implore you, Beatriz," the man's volition sounded in my brain, "my life-long peace, my life itself, is in your hands."

The girl stopped short, and wheeled about, throwing out her hands with a gesture of disdain. "Andres Molina! Are you mad?" I felt her reply. "Was it for this you opened the door of my room? I thought I had found a friend in you—the confessor of my mother; I thought you condemned this worldly, wicked scheme of hers to wed me to old Díaz, and that you had brought me here to take counsel as to how we should persuade her to change her mind. Instead, you use this clandestine meeting to tell me that you love me. You! A priest! A friar! Holy Mary! How evil a thing must I be that I can inspire so base a passion?"

"But listen, Beatriz. I have loved you so long—even in your childhood, before I took the vows, I loved you ever. That makes a difference. It is not as if this had begun beneath the frock of the priest. You do not love me? You must! You shall! For what other purpose did I counsel your mother to bring you here to the care of the good sisters? I had no way to speak with you at home—you chose another confessor—you always were self-willed! Ah, sweet! From now on I shall confess you—and of most tender sins. We will flee—to an island—to a desert—us alone where there in some solitude."

He threw his arms around her with a quick, impassioned movement. But the girl freed herself with a sudden wrench, stepping backward. They had come close to the fountain; I could see her hand gleam white, as she leaned upon it on the dark stone rim, and the glitter of a great diamond upon her finger. The long dark cloak she wore fell to her feet, and I could see her clearly in the brilliant moonlight—a creature of passing beauty, garbed in the Manola costume of Andalusia. "She has come from some masked ball," I said to myself; "they have taken her from the dance to seclude her in the convent." Even at the distance I was, and but by moonlight, I could tell the look of scorn and repulsion on her face, as she looked at the priest.

"Dastard! False friend!" she stung; "dishonored priest. This is indeed too much. My mother shall know the teachings that you offer!"

Standing over against her, the priest's handsome, dark browed countenance underwent a change—the change from one fierce passion to another.

"You threaten me, little fool? Betray me to your mother! But that dear mother is beata—a devotee. Already your little piety has terrified and estranged her. She sees you as a brand amid the burning. If I should tell her tomorrow the devil carried you bodily away for your sins she would not question. She has a convenient faith in miracles, you see!"

"What then? Indeed, I know her weakness all too well. I have a stronger stay. Am I a child—a poor, weak creature like the women here—your Mexican creoles, who submit to whatever yoke is laid upon them? Remember that I am a Spanish woman—we Andaluces have wills of our own. Bah! I let myself be brought to the convent, to gain time. Have you forgotten that there is an old law by which lovers may appeal from the restraints imposed by arbitrary parents, to the aid of justice, which reunites them, if no unlawful obstacle exists? While I have been here in sanctuary, where I had hopped to gain your influence to mollify my mother, my lover has invoked this law in our behalf."

"Your—lover? Accepted—lover?"

The girl smiled with some malice. "Even so. You did not know? Why then, it would appear that my good mother, for all her blind devotion, lacked somewhat of confidence toward her dear confessor. My lover? Yes! So true, so noble, so deeply loved, that other men beside seem all like ghosts. Here was cause enough that I should despise your suit, even though it involved not the monstrous thought of sacrilege. You dare to turn your eyes where León worships?"

Then, even as I heard through the silence the sense of their unspoken word, I saw through the darkness, as before, the movements that befell. I saw the priest strike down the girl with a brutal, coward blow, and then stand like a man dazed by the sight of what he had done. I saw him flee away to the inner regions of the convent, casting behind him guilty, frightened glances, and presently return, bearing where with to conceal the evidences of his sin. I saw him pry up and lift aside the great stone flags in the centre of the fountain, and lay the dead girl in the hollow he formed beneath them, laying the basalt slabs again in place. I even noted the murky state of the water. Then he slipped away into the shadows of the church, and the fountain plashed as ever, and the mocking-bird sang on.

Part 2

Early the following day I received a call. My visitor was a priest—a Cuban Spaniard, whom I had long known as the Cura of Pachuca. He was a short, plump, rosy, pleasant man, with the softest hands, the gentlest voice, and the kindliest eyes imaginable. A true churchman, too was he; that is to say, a thorough man of the world, using tactfully all knowledge and experience to the glory of his faith and its proliferation, yet never obtruding his religious beliefs and missions; merry, philosophical, with tastes inclined toward literature and art—such was the Cura Santa Lucía. I welcomed no guest more gladly, and his company was particularly grateful this day, when I was in a state of mind half dreaminess, half exaltation, from the experience of the night.

"I am going to be your neighbor," said the good priest, presently, when we had chatted awhile of indifferent things; "Yes, I have been appointed to the curacy of El Sagrado Corazón."

I was very sincerely pleased—from selfish reasons—for

I was glad to be able to see more of the Cura. Glad from more altruistic motives, knowing what a difficulty it must have been for this clever, scholarly man with his fine social gifts, had been a stay in the mountains, surrounded by rude and brawling miners.

"Truthfully, I did not like it out there. It did not make me happy. Yet, take it how you will, it is a good world this. I know none better."

Favorite stock phrases of the Cura, such were the words he now spoke in answer to my observations regarding the change. From this, nothing was easier than to pass to the subject of the church of his duties, its rich, aristocratic congregation, and the special privileges enjoyed by the guild. Many of these advantages, the Cura went on to say, had accrued to that particular benefice through the energy and holiness of a priest whose duty as chaplain of the convent, and in various other positions of dignity and trust, had been at the middle of the seventeenth century. The zeal and ability of this cleric -- for he had risen to high ecclesiastic rank -- had been themes for many glorifying records in the archives of the church.

"I have just been reading up in them," the Cura said, "for surely it becomes me to know the history of my living. Among the rest is a very curious story of a miracle," he went on, with a odd twinkle in his bright eyes, "a miracle performed by this holy and austere brother, Friar Andres Molina."

I started at the name.

"There was a widow in Mexico then," the priest went on, "a Spaniard—an Andalusian with one child. This daughter, Beatriz, was a brilliant girl, with independent notions of her own that interfered with the mother's proposition. Therefore, La Manola, as she was called from always wearing the Andalusian garb, was promised in marriage to an elderly man named Díaz, and resisting the match, she was imprisoned here in the convent of this church, where Friar Andres Molina prayed with and for her, until, pronouncing her an accursed thing, and invoking the devil to come and take his own, her cell was thrown open—and found to be empty."

The good Father concluded his recital with an indulgent smile, then: "We of the clergy are not less than human," he said, "and Friar Andres Molina doubtless was in innocent collusion with one of the lovers of Doña Beatriz; for she appears to have had suitors galore. Indeed, the record farther states, as an evidence of her wicked power over men, that one León Aviles killed himself at the gates of the convent, as soon as the fact of her disappearance was verified."

"León! It was for the jealousy of him that she was slain!" I said. And the Cura looked at me as if doubting my sanity. Then, because I knew the liberal mind of the man, and his tolerance of theories that many would deem heretical, I told him the story of my visions of the night. He seemed not incredulous, not greatly surprised.

"These are mysterious phrases in this life of ours," he said, "and strange, inscrutable happenings. Moreover, in those half barbarous days, the men of the cassock too often abused their power. What is the day of the month that the water becomes undrinkable in the fountain?"

I started to my feet. "I had forgotten, having slept late when once I fell asleep. But—I think it must be today."

And in soon the tank was overflowing its brim, and no busy movements went on in the little square.

"For the curiosity of it, I will look up the record," said the priest, "and see if this phenomenon coincides with the miraculous disappearance of Beatriz. And if it be possible, an examination shall be made beneath the fountain."

I know not what pretext the good priest made, nor what pressure he brought to bear. Only there is one of the ministers, whose Semitic countenance bespeaks all the subtleties of diplomacy, who is deeper in fellowship with the clergy than he would care to have the Liberal party know, and it is more than likely his influence was invoked. I only know the Cura knocked at my door at an advanced hour of the night.

"Do you care to come? Shall we call up some of your American friends to accompany you?" he said. "The dates --

you understand me—coincide. I am interested beyond belief. Moreover, if that is true that we suspect, those poor relics of humanity should have Christian burial. The neighbors are asleep, and the watchmen have their instructions. Will you come?"

We woke from their chamber-door staunch, practical John Cavanaugh, and a slim young attaché of the diplomatic corps, and, wrapped in waterproofs, for a cold, small rain was misting down, we made our way through the courtyard and the shadowy great zaguán, Señor del Río, the administrator, himself giving us egress, that we might not arouse the hall porter, to wonder at and perhaps to spy on our movements. The men chosen for the work were on the ground, and the plashing stream of the Pila stilled, and its basin drained of the water. Even the cement between the lozas was already picked out, and all awaited the arrival of the Cura. The watchman from the corner had drawn near, and curiously watched the scene. The Cura gave the word; the crowbars were inserted, slowly the levers worked, and the great slabs were upraised and lifted aside. The workmen—people of the Cura, he had brought with him to the country—caught their breath at what they half saw in the dim light, with a cry of fear. But religious feeling and respect for their priest triumphed over the natural impulse of horror and superstition, and they quietly stepped aside, removed their broad brimmed hats, and held the lanterns nearer. Clear in the yellow light, we saw there plainly, resting in a hollow of the damp and noisome earth, as in a cradle, the form of a woman, young, and of surpassing beauty. Her rich raiment was unstained, and her face and delicate hands looked as if she had been laid there a moment since, and not two centuries ago. It was the hapless girl whose lovely face and Manola garb I had plainly seen through the darkness of the night, and whose sweet brave words, all unspoken, I had heard. The Cura stooped, and lifted a silken cover from a chest of ancient Spanish cedar, marvelously carved.

"We will lay her in here."

With one accord, he and the Americans bent to take up the beauteous figure that no menial hands should profane. But at their touch, it crumbled away swiftly as fades a dream, and there lay but a handful of moldy dust, with a great sparkling diamond glittering in the midst.

CITY OF MEXICO, June, 1887.

Yda H. Addis

The Picture of the Priest

Appeared *The Argonaut*, June 15, 1891, part 2, June 22, 1891

During the space of a good many weeks, I had been reading in the local press of Mexico City such comments as the following: "In a sumptuous home, in one of the most elegant and spacious streets of this our magnificent city of The Great Tenochtitlan, there is the home of a lady, who at one time was famous for her beauty. This splendid woman fabulously wealthy, her palatial home filled with choice furniture and costly luxuries evidenced by the well-known refinement and elegance of taste peculiar to the Mexican character, yet this lady is not happy—far from it. No! A dreadful secret hangs over her and a frightful affliction obscures her existence. In the dead silence of the night, when insomnia visits and bids her to watch the slow retreat of the lagging hours, at the same ominous moment of the night, and every night, an awful phantom visits, with staring eyes and pallid countenance, and, wearing his blood-stained clothing, he moves through her gorgeous home until he reaches the room wherein she may be at the moment; and, as her eyes rest upon the specter, she fall fainting before it. We have not heard any explanation for the remarkable demonstration."

Such was the general tone of the local journals, which are, indeed, but sorry types of newspapers for the most part, their grandiloquence and fulsome stories strongly in need of providing news, and with a general slipshodness lack of accuracy. With regard to the subject in question, there was an occasional slight variety of item; once it was stated in the *Diario del Hogar* that the haunted lady was offering large sums of money to women who would stay with her at night because her servants, one and all, positively refused to remain past nightfall in her house on account of its ghostly visitant. Again, it was announced that she would allow neither man nor child upon her premises, only adult women; and later yet, comment was made upon the circumstance that the police were called in to prevent the intrusion upon this unfortunate lady's privacy by curiosity-mongers, who, during the daylight hours, had broken into her home demanding to inspect the haunted house. But withal, there was no definite clue to the mystery, albeit the subject acquired a certain social importance and was discussed with some languid degree of interest. Some stated that the scene of the apparition was a house near the grim old Inquisition building, theatre of so many bygone horrors, now used as quarters of the National School of Medicine. Others assigned its location near the innumerable ex-convents of the city.

I was very much interested. Born without the slightest belief in the supernatural, yet this subject had always possessed for me the strangest and most powerful charm. During the earlier post-bellum years, I had been surrounded by the Negroes who had been slaves of my family, and from them I had heard a long succession of tales of grisly marvels. Then the nurse who had longest charge of my unruly childhood was a Cornish woman, and many a night when my mother was not at home due to the sea of social duties, satisfied that her naughty child was safe in the care of sedate, faithful Ellen, that insensitive minister, having attended to all my physical needs, carefully complying with my mother's insistence that no light must be on in my bedroom, yet that Ellen must be with me—this ingenious woman gratified her social instincts by assembling her fellow-servants in the adjoining room, where, during their sewing or needle-work, she entertained them with stories of her native land, fearful traditions of the moors and wolds, ghastly histories of the undersea mines, and of monstrous crimes, all of which bathed in the cold sweat of horror the poor little listener, cowering there in terror with no other consolation than the strip of penumbral light through the door ajar, and afraid to show herself awake, lest that poor comfort be shut away from her.

But, oddly enough, the result of all this devotion of our faithful, conscientious, judicious servant was an unconquerable interest and fascination in this subject, yoked with a most persistent but unprejudiced skepticism.

All my life long a constant seeker I had been after some personal experience, but my quest had been almost pitifully fruitless. Every strange appearance that I hoped might prove to be the desired apparition, had resolved itself into some most commonplace, and, alas! at times even comical, effect. Every séance that I attended proved uneventful, except on two or three discomfiting occasions, when the finger of the faithful was turned against me as a skeptical and opposing influence. Yet the old fascination was upon me as strongly as ever; yes, even stimulated by my reading as corresponding member of a Society for Psychical Research, whose records certainly presented some curious phenomena. Given this frame of mind, it was certainly very trying to find my investigations futile, as are those of most seekers after definite facts in Mexico.

One night—it was the twelfth of December, the day of Guadalupe, patroness of Mexico—I had gone with some friends to offer the compliments of the day to their kinswoman, a Guadalupe. There had been a death in the family—either of a distant relative or some friend of the clan, and the consequent complimentary mourning exacted by the rigorous customs of the country precluded the social dance and festiveness usual on this occasion, and our hostess was agitated by the privation. She was a merry little woman, and passionately fond of dancing, for all the sadness of her delicate, sharp face and great, black eyes; so merry and jolly, indeed, was she, that her character was a continual anomalous surprise, as compared with the inane languor of the conventional Mexican lady. On the night in question, her whimsical attitude of grievance and protest kept all of us, her guests, amused. "But, indeed, it is entirely too silly," she declared, in answer to some bit of raillery; "we Mexicans are slaves to custom—and foolish customs, more often than not. I like the straightforward, the practical independence of the Americans. No! Adelaida, you need not make me your way for the compliment. I mean what I say. Your countrymen may be brusquer than we, but I think they have more sincerity and less sham. Do you think an American would let his greatest day of the year—his own feast-day—be made a disappointment by the death of the brother-in-law of a third cousin of his godfather? Why, Pancho and I barely knew Don Pepe Herrera; we had seen him not more than twice, in our lives! Is not, then, our mourning for him almost a mockery? Bah! We sit here gabbing, and mincing, and sipping a glass of wine with a ghastly pretense of enjoyment, when we might have been so merry.

"Come! Come! Lupe," said her tall, handsome husband, grave and kindly; "you are making our guests feel uncomfortable. Let's stop complaining, and each one vote upon some way of passing an hour or two. Why, your face is long enough to pass for the lady haunted by the friar. What, Adelaida! You have heard something of that matter?—You are interested?—You'd like to know more concerning it? Why, then, by the terms of my proposition, you are casting your vote for the telling ghost-stories as our substitute *pasatiempo* for dancing. What do you say? Is not this a reasonable wish? Is it passed?"

And so, by the courtesy of the company, in another moment I was asking Pancho Contreras with eager questions about his happy allusion to the mystery I had so long and vainly hunted.

The result proved to be, in one sense, incommensurate with my joy at discovering the clue; for Francisco Contreras himself knew little that was definite. It was true that Gertrudis Solis—the haunted woman—received no masculine visitors; and, while the timid women of this family were on visiting terms with her, they would prefer to brave the terrors of purgatory than enter her home except during the broadest light of day. Indeed, that they ever set foot in the haunted house at all was due to the aforesaid constraints of strict Mexican etiquette. Therefore, all that Pancho Contreras could tell me was purely on hearsay.

On the other hand, it was much to learn, as he was able to assure me, that there was no doubt as to the authenticity of the ghost. That the details were not more accurately known was due, it was evident, to the natural sensitiveness of the afflicted woman and to her denial of the facts in self-protection against the morbidly curious. It was known that she had made a pilgrimage to Rome, to obtain Papal absolution for some crime, as it was supposed, connected with her mysterious trouble; and it was understood that the "Santo Papa" had imposed upon her some very severe penalties.

Perhaps what most impressed me in what I was hearing was the statement that Gertrudis Solis had been a nun in her girlhood, before the reform laws abolished convents in Mexico. "And, whether the specter exists or not," concluded Pancho Contreras, "hers is certainly a very awful fate, since she passes her nights alone, convinced, whether rightly or not, of its actual existence."

"But—but—" I stammered in my eagerness—"is it possible that no one—no one—can be found to stay with her? You say she offers large gratuities—people will do almost anything for money, and there are so many dreadfully poor people in Mexico."

"And some of them have gone to her, tempted by her generous offers. And each and every one has seen, or claimed to see, the same awful sight that she sees—the sight of a mangled, bleeding friar—and like her, each one has swooned with the horror of it."

"I wonder," I said, with considerable doubt and distrustfulness, "if she would let me stay with her—a stranger and a foreigner?"

"Adelaida! The ghost—friar might kill you!" said pretty, rosy Maria; and "Pass a night in that house!" shrilled nervous Guadalupe, "never! You know I love you, *vieja*, yet I'm sure that not even to save your life could I stay in that house!"

"But—oh! She does not mean it," declared gentle Elena; and the rest, young men and all, joined the startled chorus.

Only serious, placid Pepita, the mother of Maria and Elena, seemed not astonished. "Be still, my coward daughters. You must remember your friend has had another sort of education different from here. And yes; be sure she means this. Have you forgotten that she always sleeps by choice in the haunted room at the home of the Valencias in Querétaro?—that room where unseen hands drag off the coverings from the sleeper, and where a luminous face gleams out in the midst of the darkness?"

"And by the same token, I never had more peaceful, undisturbed slumbers," I said, stoutly; "no—it is clear that my only chance of seeing the ghost I have been all my life seeking is here in the house of your friend. Will you introduce me to her? Please try to arrange for me to spend the night there? Oh, thank you, thank you! Lupe, shall we now play forfeits?" And in my exultant delight I introduced into that mild game so many audacious and startling novelties that Guadalupe declared herself almost consoled for the lack of dancing.

So it came about that, a few days later, I was introduced, in company with Pepita, her daughters, and Guadalupe, into the sala, or reception-room, of Gertrudis Solis—a great room, furnished stiffly and formally, after the Mexican tradition, with an abundance of rich, elegant furniture and not without a few costly trifles of knick knackery, but overall dull, comfortless, and forbidding. Gertrudis Solis received us eagerly—I might say warmly, if so confident a term could be compatible with the wistfulness of her manner and her self-repression, as of one long accustomed to subdue all impulses at the domination of an imperative necessity. She was a woman certainly of more than fifty years old, as I knew she must be from her history, yet in a light not too strong she might readily have passed for half that age, so clear, so fine and delicate was her fair complexion, so little touched with silver her smoothly braided hair, so lustrous were her great dark eyes. This was, indeed, a beautiful countenance, yet one with something of the fearful. I could but think of the crimson sparks of coals gleaming through the dead white of ashes; even the gruesome suggestion of a galvanized corpse came to me, as I gazed upon her, so striking was the effect of smoldering passions straining through the strange immobility which comes to characterize the faces of those long used to conventual's seclusion.

The preliminary explanations had all been made by our mutual friends beforehand, and our reception was that a well-bred woman accords to visitors under ordinary conditions. Before my companions left, we were ushered into the dining-room, where was spread a tempting supper, and here, for the first time, Gertrudis Solis referred to the abnormal conditions. "The hour, I know, is inopportune," she said; "but my people all leave the house before nightfall. It is arranged"— to me— "that we may have refreshment during the night, if it so please you."

The four Mexican guests were manifestly disturbed as night was fast approaching, and our hostess observed this and with graceful tact dismissed them. When we were alone together, I laid my hand on the cold hand of Gertrudis Solis, and said: "I hope you, trust me. I've come here to help you, if it be in my power. I am neither timid nor nervous, and I have undergone hardships and perils enough to confirm my self-possession. I am prepared for defense or resistance, active or passive. See my practical provisions," and I threw open a hand-bag wherein I had a bottle of cognac, some simple remedies for syncope or hysteria, an excellent revolver, and half-a-dozen of the brightest and breeziest of modern novels and nonsense-books.

"Where," I said, "shall we await the—the manifestation?"

She reflected for a moment. "I will take you to my chamber."

It was a very large sleeping-room, comfortably, even luxuriously, furnished, and as I entered I looked around at first in curiosity, I thought that the Papal penalty at least would involve the relinquishment of bodily comforts.

Gertrudis Solis drew me forward to the bedside. "The work of keeping this room in order is done by my own hands," she said; "no other human being has entered here since the Holy Father assigned my penance—since he ordered me to keep THAT ever hanging before me!" She pointed to the wall opposite the foot of the narrow brass bed, and suddenly lifted the waxed candles high so that they threw their light just where the gaze of the bed's tenant would naturally fall on waking.

There hung a life-size painting—I do not see how I can

describe it. Words seem inadequate to convey the details, depicted, as it did, the vagueness and obscurity of a darkened room, on whose wall was dimly distinguished a great crucifix and a holy water shell at the head of a narrow, conventual's bed. But, oh! The realistic horror of what lay on that austere couch! It was the figure of a man in the garb of a priest, the clothing greatly disordered. The face was clear-cut, and the general correctness of the features was strangely at variance with the sensual lines that character graves into fixed expressions, and with the coarse, brutal mouth, unfailing mark of the Spanish priesthood in Mexico. I believe that every beholder, looking as I did on that painted dead face, must say to himself, as I did: "This is the portrait of a man stricken down in the commission of some awful crime, whose taint, sinking into his corpse, gives it an added horror." The throat, the arms, and the breast of the body were bare, over the heart was a wide, gaping stab-wound, and upon the throat and breast were other frightful gashes that seemed to have been cut with purposeless, frenzied violence. But the unspeakable repulsiveness of it all was that the wounds and the whole body showed more than the beginning of mortal corruption. Long study at the galleries of San Carlos and familiarity at local studios had taught me what cunning use the Mexican School of painters' make of the pigment bitumen in flesh tints. (Is not the wondrous coloring of the dead

Indian in Parra's[i] great painting a proof of this practice?) But the ghastly hues of this putrescence surely could have been laid on with no mineral substance—this was animal matter itself. I could not trust my sense of sight for such fearful realism; it seemed to me this must be some unnatural effect of candle-light. But, even as I looked, in front of the theatre across the street the intense electric-light leaped into brilliant glow, and that sincere, searching light blazed through the open windows, its distinctness and revelation making the realism tenfold greater. Gertrudis Solis quickly closed the curtains. And, indeed, it might have been dangerous to see, under certain condition, from across the way, that fearful figure.

"Do you dare," she said, tremulously, "remain with me here—in that presence?"

"I will stay here," I answered, and sat down in an easy-chair, where I could gaze upon the picture. And—here is a strange phase of human nature—when I spoke, it was with abject fear and only under the coercion of strong, determined pride and stubborn protest against succumbing; but as I gazed, the instinct of the artist so overcame those lower impulses that all my reluctance vanished or was absorbed in marveling admiration of the skill that had delineated that picture.

"Then this will be the first time that I watch here not

alone," said Gertrudis Solis; "the—the others—the people who have come to watch with me have always remained in the sala; without knowing what this room held, they shrunk from its mystery and would not enter. But then—." She spoke now with a sudden access of patrician pride and confidence, "they were either menials or sordid souls, who came from motives of interest instead of courage and sympathy."

I remarked that a change had come over her, as if, in companionship of an equal plane, she had found strength and courage. Somewhat of animation was in her manner, in her movement, her expression, her intonation. She no longer cast tremulous, furtive looks about her, and she looked at the terrible canvas full and directly instead of turning upon it a sidelong regard, as when she stood with me before it. And it was with a changed voice—with tones that rang resolve and protest—that she spoke to me again.

"If you will hear it," she said, I will tell you my story. And for the first time, barring only what I told to the head of the church at Rome." It struck me as somewhat strange that she should say "the head of the church"—and at that, not "my" nor "our" church, but "the church at Rome"—instead of using the customary term "his holiness."

I told her how gladly I would listen, and she continued at once, with a certain pitiful eagerness.

"You can not dream," she said, "what your coming here

has done for me. From the moment Pepita spoke of your offer, I have been like another woman. I was afraid to yield to the impression, lest, after all, you should fail me—you see, I had not seen you and did not know you. But I had been so long alone, abandoned to my fate and my curse. I have in Mexico many who call themselves my friends, and even some who are bound to me by blood-ties. But not one came forward ever to my rescue. Because they knew nothing definite of my story, they showed me just so much scant surface courtesy as was exacted by convention and by the knowledge that, after all, I must die some day, and dying, must devise to some one my large possessions. But if one had known the truth, never again might I have looked upon any. Think of it! Can you figure to yourself what an unendurable thing it has been to go on bearing my burden alone for all these long years? If I could have told my secret—what a relief! What a comfort! But to tell it would be to sever my last tie and contact with humanity. But you have come to help me, full of divine compassion for a suffering woman! I bless the foreign customs, the broad-minded, pure-hearted independence that gives you, young and alone, the courage to do this noble, generous, grand deed!"

How shall I describe my abashed humiliation and shame as this poor, suffering soul thus imputed such lofty purpose to an act that I knew was inspired in my heart by no motive worthier than a morbid interest, a trivial and unlovely curiosity.

"You have brought me new hope, new life," went on the poor, sad creature; "I am almost frightened at its power— it makes me rebellious. For the first time in all these years I have questioned the justice of the sentence that condemned me to suffer all the years of my life in silence and in solitude. Since Pepita came to me and told me of the offer of a foreigner, I have been reading all that I could find concerning your nation, and I have found—oh! so much of encouragement. No one could know better than I know that my crime was monstrous; but it has not been hidden by the secluded life I have led, not only wretched for myself, but hopeless and useless to others. Oh! I might have made some atonement! My wealth is great—how much misery I might have relieved with it—how many struggling beings I might have helped to live lives of hope, and use, and honor! Surely, surely, there must be something amiss, not only in the social code, but in the religion of the country where such a sacrifice can be imposed. Now hear my story and judge me:

"I was the youngest child and only unmarried daughter of my parents when, at the time I was between eighteen and nineteen years old, the clergy beset my family with insistence that I should become a nun. My brothers and sisters all were married, and it was urged that fidelity to the church could be best shown by devoting to her service at least one member of the family. I have often wondered how much zeal was involved in this insistency and how much of it hinged upon my fortune, which would accrue to the church upon my taking the veil. Of late, too—and it is most strange that I did not sooner reflect on what has gone far to extenuate my conduct in my own eyes—of late I have thought with great suspicion that the heaviest pressure brought to bear upon my parents was exercised by a young priest"—she looked up at the fearful picture, and shuddered with a strong convulsion of repulsion—"and his insistence grew harsher and more imperative when it became known that I was betrothed—oh! Tito, my beloved!" She buried her face in her hands and shook with anguish; but when she raised her face again; her eyes were hot and tearless.

"Oh! I rebelled against those tyrannical forces with all the passionate strength of my being! I was young and full of life, and the world said I was beautiful; to this plea came the answer that I should devote myself to God in gratitude for his gifts. I had from childhood given tireless study to art, and I had bright dreams of a famous future wherein I should equal or surpass La Sumaya; to this, a remark that the most noted work of that gifted woman was of San Sebastian over the Altar of Pardon at the cathedral, and I was reminded that eternal glory, beyond worldly fame, would be mine, a reward for the paintings of saints, martyrs, and apostles which I should paint and then give to the holy church. I pleaded my affection for my family—I was told that the only way to prove it lay in encompassing their salvation, only jeopardized by my obstinacy. I declared my undying love for Tito Arríala, and my determination never to give him up. He was immediately sent on an official mission to Tampico, where yellow fever was raging, and where he died of the disease within a fortnight. In short—was there ever a case where a Mexican woman could do nothing but to yield to submission?—At last, I was forced to succumb.

"My novitiate was dreary, but free enough from active distress—it was only after I had taken the black veil, and was irrevocably pledged, that there began a frightful persecution. Do not think that I mean to insult that noble, self-sacrificing band of women who devote themselves to good deeds—no doubt I admire their integrity in general. But—in Mexico, at that time—the clergy was very corrupt and its power mighty. The priest, Joaquín Gonzaga—he whose urgency to my sacrifice had been so stringent—was a nephew of the mother superior of our convent, and he visited often. Whether to facilitate his ends or to avert scandal from her own community, I do not know, but she presently had me transferred to another house, where Gonzaga was the confessor, and here his position gave him every advantage.

By day and by night, at my work—for they set me to painting altar-pieces—in lonely corridors, at prayers, even before the very altar, his insistence plagued me, his gross looks made my blood boil with rage. Rebuke, reproach, reminder of the vows of his office—meant nothing—neither did scorn or disdain do more than fan his passion to hotter excess. Meanwhile, however, I had found a protector and companion. This was an old lay sister, Anastasia, whose task it was to scrape smooth and clean the red-brick tiles of the floors, and it was the most onerous tasks that the nuns avoided. She was believed to be weak-minded; in reality she feigned, for her own purposes, a mental unsoundness, and this trait did her good service in my behalf, because she could be with me in times of danger. Her love for me was something indescribable, and for many long weeks its vigilance stood between me and evil.

"The interior government of our house was more than arbitrary, and I could only obey when the superior ordered me to move to a cell in a remote part of the great building, around an angle at the end of a lonely hallway. My new room, which had an alcove, was far more spacious than the regular cells, and this, with the arrangement of its light, made it, as the superior observed, more suitable for my use of painting. My one resource, my one refuge, had been to seclude myself in my cell sometimes for days with the excuse

I was absorbed in my work, and this privilege had been given me in view, I suppose, of the great amount of work I accomplished, for I painted with a feverish rapidity and the work so done had a life and a strength far beyond what I painted under normal conditions.

It seemed to me that I would enjoy greater freedom, greater security in this new cell, because of its isolation. The first night that I spent there—oh, God! Oh, God! How can a woman undergo such an ordeal and live to tell of it?—That night I awoke at the grasp of a hand upon my throat, and my eyes opening looked up into the devilish face of Gonzaga. Silenced and half-strangled as I was, I fought him desperately, but he was strong and muscular, and I was but a weak and slender woman, and I fainted from fright and exhaustion. When I returned to consciousness, my poor old Anastasia was there, snarling with despair and fury, and Gonzaga, holding her two poor, withered, old wrists in one of his strong hands, was taunting her with having come too late to save me. I was frantic with despair and shame, with pain and dishonor. Anastasia was accustomed to carry in her belt her scraping tool; you know—you have seen the straight-edged, broad, clumsy knife that the scrub-women use for tile-scrapers? I saw it gleaming there, and I snatched it and plunged it into the priest's body. The first blow must have killed him for I struck his heart; but I was like a madwoman, and I gashed and stabbed the body until Anastasia, full of horror, dragged me away. Four days the dead man lay there on my bed; in those four days the old pretext served us well to exclude the nuns, who marveled greatly, Anastasia brought me word, at the prolonged absence of the confessor. For once my excuse was a just one; in those four days I painted that canvas, impelled by I know not what morbid motive. And we were distressed to know how to dispose of that decaying body, which already poisoned our atmosphere and would presently make known the crime to those about us."

She paused, and I was conscious that her voice for some minutes had been faltering and that her face was pallid to ghastliness. Her hands were fluttering feebly, as if resisting her efforts to hold still.

"You are ill!" I said, or tried to say, but I had the strange, impotent sensation which one feels while vainly endeavoring to call out while in a nightmare. I felt, too, that numbness was creeping over me with a strange corporeal lightness. I made a strenuous effort, opened the bag, and carried the flask of cognac to my hostess. I poured a generous amount between her tremulous lips, and then, without ado, tipped up the bottle to my own mouth.

"Es inútil!" ("It is useless!") I heard Gertrudis Solis murmur. And my legs buckled beneath me, and I sank down upon the sofa.

Part 2

Of the experience that then followed I do not know how to describe. As I lay upon the couch, inert and speechless, and yet seeming to be instinct with a twofold existence, I saw the furniture of the room where we were in and so much of the lighted sala beyond as could be seen through the door; yet at the same time I seemed to be transported elsewhere and pass through a succession of scenes that I am about to go over, never merging, it must be remembered—never losing or confusing the real and present situation in the factitious occurrences. In the same way I preserved distinct identities; I was throughout the skeptic, the would-be student of the occult forces and conditions, while at the same time I saw the actions and heard the words of the people who passed—or seemed to pass—before me, and yet, by some mysterious sympathy or clairvoyance, I was one with each and all of these, entering into their very thoughts and innermost emotions. Let the philosopher, the savant, or the mystic, explain this strange inter-relationship—I but relate these things as they appeared before me.

The first of the strange scenes seemed to take up and carry forward the sorrowful history of Gertrudis Solis form the point where she had ceased speaking. I was in the narrow and gloomy confines of her convent-cell, where she stood, a woman of unspeakable beauty, not marred, indeed, by the evident traces of grief and despair, but rather vivified by that emotion into an increased charm, a spiritual loveliness almost supernatural, as she gazed upon the sight before her—the frightful figure of the dead man upon her bed, identical, line for line, with the picture before us on the wall of this chamber of a house in one of the best-known streets of modern Mexico City. I lifted to it my eyes—the only movement within my volition—at the very moment that I heard the voice of the old woman standing beside the nun.

"You must yield to me, niña of my heart!" the old woman was saying; "now that I have been—oh, God ! too late to save you from him, you must let me save you from the consequences. What would happen to you if you were to confess all and stand trial? Poor child, if that were all, some justice you might find, indeed, in the courts, some pity from the judges, when should be known the awful thing that has happened to you. And yet—it were not so easy! oh, child!" The woman's gestures grew wilder, more impassioned; she dropped the formal "usted" of respectful and ceremonious language, and continued with the tu (you) of familiarity. You do not know the perils that plague a woman that enters a Mexican prison? With your youth and beauty—forever your danger would increase a hundred-fold, and you would become fair prey for every official, from the jailor to the highest of the judges. No! No! Not even justice can be had by a woman here, save at the cost of honor! But even so much would not be granted to you! To lift a hand against a priest is to sign your own death warrant!—And a priest with such powerful connections!

"Listen! Let me tell you a story that will show you what may happen to you. Have you ever wondered why I have taken an interest in you? Twenty years ago I had a daughter, as young and beautiful as you are whose father made her take the veil at this same convent. Not unlike your story! She, too, was pursued and persecuted by the confessor of the community, and she, in defending herself, inflicted a fatal wound upon him. She had saved her honor—but at what price! That self-same night, a niche was opened in the thick wall of the convent, and my child was placed therein, and the wall rebuilt between her and the world, and she was left to a slow and fearful death there.[2] For this reason I came here as the lowest and poorest of laborers, and for this, all these years, have I pretended insanity that would enable me to kneel and pray, at whatever moment I would, before any spot that might be the tomb of my darling daughter—for I do not know where the spot is where she was buried alive. So,

---

during all these years, I have left not an inch of the walls unconsecrated, if the prayers of an unfortunate mother can prevail for a hapless victim's pardon! Thank God that my long sojourn has qualified me to give you such help as there was none to render to my daughter!

Gertrudis Solis threw her arms around the other, and laid her head upon the old woman's bosom.

"I am in your hands," she murmured; "do with me as you believe is best—my only friend! To you alone I ask for help. Even God Himself has forsaken me, because He has let this awful thing happen. What shall I do?"

"Have you not noticed," said Anastasia, "that for the past weeks a young man has been laying siege to your affection?" No! No! Why should you notice, when you have been wrapped up in memories of your dead fiancé and then the problems you have faced with the priest? But I have marked full well the young cavalier's endeavors—my faith! As well I might, since scarcely a day has passed that he has not approached me with bribes to give you his letters. Every day, when the nuns go into chapel, he is there to see if by some happy chance he can not catch a sight of you through the jealous lattice that screens the gallery given over to the *monjas*. And every day, when the services are over, he hangs about the gates in the forlorn hope of seeing you, or of prevailing on me to mediate between him and you. Now, in the extremity of our distress, I have thought of him as an instrument for you salvation, and tonight I have made a date—a tryst for you to meet him!"

But—"A tryst with a lover!" asked the poor nun; "No! Never, after what has happened to me, I dread and fear men! One and all, I'd rather take my punishment, however grisly, than consent to this!" and her sobs and shudders of protest were very pitiful. Then the woman reassured her, and at last succeeded in calming her treating her with certain herbs that seem so simple, but in reality are so potent—the knowledge of their use being, in some way, a legacy from their Aztec ancestry, possessed by few, indeed, of their descendants, but, where known, of a potency far surpassing the pharmacopoeia of modern schools.

And Anastasia went and came, sneaking in to that dismal cell items that enabled her to hide its bleakness into something of the semblance of a womanly tenancy. And she spread upon its tiny table a dainty supper and flasks of generous wines, all provided and brought by resources known only to her.

Then, when she introduced into the confines of that habitation a man, young, handsome, wearing every indication of worldly wealth and distinction, his senses were flattered by an appearance of gala attire, put on in his honor by that austere retreat, whose atmosphere was loaded with fragrant perfumes.

The man was young, hot-blooded, and deeply enamored, and not shy regarding women, yet even his eagerness and the confidence inspired by the significance of this rendezvous could not overcome the impression he received from the sadness of his nun-hostess, her timidity and shrinking, and the air of alarm and even aversion with which she met his advances.

Anastasia generously poured out into goblets to one then to the other the liquors she had brought, and more than once she slipped in the subtle Indian sedative and stimulant. And then, at last, when she judged that the herbs and the wines allied themselves with the ardor of his passion to reduce him to a state of complaisance, the old woman asked to speak to him, and related to him a skillfully garbled version of the conditions. By her astute rendering the true facts were given, supported by one or two variations that strengthened her point to their hearer; the priest's persecution, as she represented, were increased, if not inspired, by a knowledge of the love of Gertrudis for her present guest and the fear of successful rivals. The old woman took upon herself, moreover, the guilt of the murder, she having slain the man; she declared that he had more than once crossed the threshold.

"And now, caballero," she concluded, as she led the way to the alcove, "unless you aid us to avoid the consequences of my reckless deed, farewell to the happiness of yourself and this poor, innocent niña. Here you have the cause of her coyness and forbidding—she dare not display the profound love she feels for you, lest she involve you in our ruin. But I fear not so," she added, with wily flattery, "for surely a gentleman so wise, so strong and powerful, will know how to extricate us from this dilemma and secure for himself the happiness of the love of this dear niña." And with that she caught up a great shawl of Chinese crepe, magnificently embroidered, such as were popular for gala use in Mexico of those days; and, drawing it aside from where it was spread over the bed, she disclosed the corpse.

That the young man was shocked and horrified, he showed most clearly; indeed, it seemed that he would withdraw and retire from the connection. But the old woman was urgent, ingratiating, and plausible. Whatever station she had occupied in her previous life—and no word of hers, now or at any time, served to indicate it—her tact and talent, her subtlety, her knowledge of human nature, and her eloquence proved her of ability far beyond the average. She pressed the matter now with ardor, while the poor nun cowered apart, silent and crushed.

At this time, the Anti-Clerical party was waxing strong

in Mexico, and many, if not most of the men of the country, were under the impression that the men of the upper and middle classes, perhaps of the entire world, most universally, were becoming nonbelievers. Something of this reactionary feeling, no doubt, actuated the young man in question. Add to that the natural horror arising from the priest's behavior; the instinct of chivalry that's so strong a thing inspires even in a degenerate like him, but retained the impulses of a decent manhood, as opposed to him who triumphs by brute force; compassion for the hapless women; the sense of personal injury involved in the dead man's encroachment; and a characteristic dare-deviltry and love of adventure; and here are more than enough motives to explain why after a brief hesitation, the gallant threw himself at the feet of the *religiosa*, kissed her hands, and, with all the extravagant, hyperbolic rhetoric, pledged himself to her service and her rescue from the dreadful and dangerous situation that bound her.

"Be happy, then soul of my soul," he concluded; "with the same skill and secrecy with which she has brought me here, this good friend of yours will smuggle me out again, and between the two of us we will carry to the street below this carrion. Loathsome as is the task, for the love of you and your safety, I shall carry him on my shoulders to the canal of San Lázaro—happily it is not far away—and once I have dumped him in, the carcass of the zopilote, I shall hurry back here to receive my reward from your sweet lips and to plan, for the night is young, the means of your escape from this convent—hateful, jealous, yet worthy of all envy, since it holds your peerless beauty."

The he and Anastasia bound up in the rich shawl that foul an smelly burden, around it wrapped swathing of the coarse rush-mats of the country, and then they slipped stealthily away through the dark, silent corridors, to the secret entrance that the old woman knew about, while Gertrudis still crouched, frightened and wretched, where they had left her. And the shadow of her doom lay upon her; the curse of her ruined life, her lost honor, mocked and trampled; the withering blight of the companionship of these past few days, while that hateful, putrid THING lay near her—a memory to linger ineffaceable through all her life to come; the ghostly pictures imagination painted, of the dark form stealing through the black, empty, voiceless streets wherein lurked unknown dangers; its scared detours around the feeble, pallid points of lights, so insignificant in the gloom, where stood the lantern of infrequent watchmen; the exhausted, breathless halt at the barrio of San Lázaro—that somber, repellent area of narrow streets or alleys, slippery causeways, rotten bridge ways, nauseous smells, and fetid exhalations; the lowering of the shapeless, ominous load, and the startling splash as the mass should be hurled plunging into the slimy, oily black water of the stagnant ditch-way. Surely there were not thoughts to cheer or encourage the poor soul, so young, so fair, that was so full of hope, so sinless, and now, by no act or blame of her own, sunk in a black and hopeless pit of loss and shame and infamy. And for the future? The impeding return of this man, unloved, unknown, an hour ago a stranger unseen, who would claim from her the reward of the service he had undertaken at the instance of his own unworthy passion. Afterward, or discovery made infamous, or escape to a life of degradation, or the life-long imprisonment of the convent, with the worm ever gnawing at her heart, and—who could tell?—Perhaps in the future recurrent persecutions like this that had wrecked her already.

Old Anastasia came back, and slowly, deliberately began to gather up for removal to their hiding-place the fragments of the supper, the flowers, and the draperies she had smuggled in to give the apartment a festal appearance. She wore an air of elation, but there was something sinister and cruel in her aspect. Watching her tremblingly, the nun at last sprang forward and raised her hands in desperate entreaty. "Oh, spare me! Spare me! No doubt you have meant well; but his return here—as a lover—I can not, will not meet him—"

"Listen!" said the old woman, sternly; "do you have so

little trust in me—so little that you would think I would let you suffer a new wrong to come upon you? Since my daughter died, I have seen in all men foes and demons—no punishment too severe, no fate too cruel for them. As they live only for their passions, by their passions shall they be blinded and lost. No, no! To one man you have been a victim, and you shall not suffer by another. You didn't have the indifference to plan nor the power to execute. I—it is I—have saved you; and you are innocent of the crime, that is if what I have done is a crime. Do not be fearful of the eager young blade because he will not return here—he will never trouble you again. Listen, in the last glass of wine he drank,--I gave him *hierba* enough for a dozen like him. He no longer will sigh at church portals, nor ogle convent-windows. I brought him here as a tool, and I have used him. If the beverage let him go so far as San Lázaro, he is a Samson. It will not let him reach halfway coming back here!"

And, as she spoke, the convent cell shifted and quivered and darkened in its outlines, and instead of it I scanned a straitened thoroughfare between high looming walls, where a man was moving hurriedly through the darkness. He passed across a thin shadow of light, streaming from a dim lamp that burned before a saint set in a wall-niche. He was free from the burden he had taken away from the convent; he was moving uncertainly; his steps grew shorter and halted, like the steps of one benumbed or frozen, and half-a-score of paces farther on, he wavered, reeled, and fell and lay upon his face, inert and lifeless.

Then all grew dark and vague—a strange, quivering, pulsating darkness that cleared away again instantly, and I sat upon the damask sofa, well and in my normal condition, save for the slight tingling sensation, like that which follows a "foot asleep." Gertrudis Solis was looking at me in the face, with an intense eagerness and misgiving. "You have seen," she said; "you have heard. And—are you terrified?"

I reassured her, and then, still under the prompting of some force beyond my own volition, I asked her to come with me into the sala. She started to get up, but sank back weakly, trembling. I gave her some the brandy, and presently she grew stronger and passed her hand through my arm, and we moved to the door together. As we reached the threshold, "You will find it the same outside," she said, "IT is in the sala—it is everywhere." And so I found it. Close beside us walked—or slipped, or floated; I do not know the term to use for the movement of that impalpable Presence—close beside us moved the figure of the priest, with its gaping wounds and its decaying tissues, even as it was in the picture, even as it was in the visions I had seen, even as I had seen or felt it beside me in the chamber. And yet—and strange to say—I was not frightened, though surely such an apparition might scare even the bravest. But my mind was strained in wonder—seeking for a solution to the mystery. At last I became convinced—and I may as well say now that I have never found a more plausible explanation—that this grisly sight had so stamped itself upon the mind of Gertrudis Solis, in those days of fearful neighborhood and companionship with it, that it had become a permanent, perpetual memory—a sight forever present before her mental vision. And the intensity of the impression and the force of her own mind were strong that she could transmit the impression to those about her; it was during the night in the quiet that became favorable to their reception. The likelihood of this theory she agreed upon. For, while we still stood in the sala, neither of us no longer fearful of the ghost that was close beside us. We became armed by the philosophical reflections occupying our minds. Suddenly there clanged from a clock-tower that was near the house the hour of midnight. In so short a time had transpired the visions of this night!

At the sound of the clock, Gertrudis Solis sank to her knees and for a time prayed fervently. And as she prayed, the apparition faded and vanished.

My hostess arose from her knees as one who has performed an imperative duty.

"It is," she said, "a part of my penance to pray for the soul of the dead every night at midnight. And when I have done so, I find that I can put aside my troubles and find relief and rest again until the next return of darkness."

Doesn't my theory, the power of the mind?

"Let me finish, briefly, my story," she said, when we had returned to the bedroom, "I have a strong premonition that I shall have no other opportunity to do so and to entrust to you a commission. The city rang with the sensation caused by the discovery of the corpse of him whom Anastasia had made our instrument. I do not name him, for he was of a distinguished family, and his sisters, his widow and two children, infants at the time of his death, still live here. Not many months after the events that you have heard and seen, the Laws of the Reform abolished monasteries and convents in this republic, and my poor Anastasia and I passed to the outer world again. For a while we kept in seclusion. When I once more faced old acquaintances, I discovered that an epidemic had swept away every member of my immediate family, and their property reverted to me. Wasn't this like a mockery of destiny? Nerves shattered, broken in health, bereft of family I was, and when Anastasia died from the torments of my memories, all became unbearable. The traditions—the superstitions, if you will—of my childhood forced me to confess; I traveled to Rome, to profess to the head of the church and to receive absolution from him. One of the conditions he laid upon me was the perpetual presence of that picture as a reminder of what I had done. Another was that I should speak to no man—and this, God knows! was no penance, but rather a shield and a support to my own resolution, since I have found the love of men at best but selfish passion, and only the friendship of women true, devoted, and without self-interest. This possibility was designed, no doubt, as a guard against the possibility of my marriage—a precaution idle and unneeded. As to the banishment of children from my presence, surely"—a spasm of agony distorted her face—"surely that needs no explanation. And these are the simple and natural reasons for what has seemed to all who know me so mysterious. Alone, night after night, for all these years, I have sat in wretchedness and silence, until I could not longer endure it, and since there were none to come to my aid for the sake of friendship, I was forced to pay for my companionship. To such an offer only the common and ignoble responded, and such, being fortified by no light of spirituality or of intellect, succumbed at once to mad frightening horror and fainted outright at the first glimpse of the bloody ghost. Further than this no one has seen, and none have understood. It needed a soul of another to penetrate behind the veil of earthly ignorance that obscures the relations between mind and mind—between mind and matter. But, look! The dawn is breaking. I have one thing more to tell you—one service to ask of you."

She opened a quaint old cabinet and took from it a packet of papers, formidable with the seals and official stamps that characterize legal document in Mexico.

"The last man to whom I have spoken was the attorney who drew up for me these papers—the leading lawyer of this capital. I had Papal dispensation to meet him—it would not have been granted had I admitted my purpose, for these papers give, away from the church, to the heirs of the man who lost his life in my service, an inheritance. For expediency, the deeds are not of testament but of transfer, and every precaution has been taken to insure their validity, and even this long after their execution. Once I am gone, I can not protest against their destruction and the frustration of my plans regarding them. Will you promise me to delivery them at once to the address I will write upon them?"

When I had given the promise and laid the packet within the little satchel, "Now let us go," she said, "into the sala. I wanted Pepita and Guadalupe to come, and I asked them to arrive very early, in case you should need them, after the night's ordeal."

Truly enough they came, almost at once, ushered in by the serving-women, who had a key to the outer entrance. Taking my cue from my hostess, I made no comment upon the happenings of the night, and the rigorous Mexican etiquette forbids any display of curiosity.   Chatting upon indifferent, trivial matters, we sat while old Petra prepared the morning chocolate. For my own part the developments of the night were less conspicuous in my thought than the marveling sense of admiration of this woman, whose mind was so sharp, whose reason was so lucid, whose demeanor so composed, after an experience that might well have unhinged the mind of any woman. I'm sure that the isolation alone and the mental rust and dry-rot would have sufficed in my own case.

"I have not felt so well for years," she said to Pepita; "the long conversation with our little friend has worked like a tonic to me. Oh, how they are strong, and free, and wise!—these Americanas!   Never will our own country become civilized, never take the place first world nations, until our countrywomen shall be placed upon a higher plane, no longer used as slaves or playthings, but as rational beings, insured a true respect, and honor, and protection."

Spoken earnestly, without emotions; and now she leaned back on the cushions, with her hands lightly folded, a very picture of peace, tranquility, and rest.   The others followed, and it was some moments before we turned again to look at Gertrudis. Her eyes were closed, a faint smile parted her lips, and she was very pallid. Pepita laid a hand upon her, and then, always calm and self-possessed, even in this sharp alarm, she called a servant and asked her fetch a physician.

"Meanwhile," she said, "let us lay her upon the bed and disrobe her."

We had crossed the threshold of the bedroom before I remembered what a shock awaited my companions—THE PICTURE! But as I lifted my eyes to it, I saw nothing but a gray film of charred ash that still kept the shape and even the texture of the canvas, and with the vibration of our movement, or the slight stirring of the air, it jarred from the frame and sifted down, sprinkling, with a thick fall, the form of the dead woman.

SANTA BARBARA, June, 1891.

Yda H. Addis

Addis's Note:
The discovery is frequent in Mexico of such niches in walls of convents, and even of churches, wherein are found skeletons of women—unfortunate prototypes of Constance de Beverly and Anastasia's daughter. The present writer has hastened to see opened not a few such ghastly receptacles. That the occupants were alive when entombed is clearly shown by the distorted condition of the remains. Sometimes, beside the larger frame, is found that of a very young infant. The Museo Nacional, in Mexico, contains the bodies—in this case mummified—of a woman, evidently once of exquisite shape, and an infant, taken from the wall of a church in that city.—Y. H. A.

Above: The Trial of Constance de Beverly
by Toby Edward Rosenthal
Source: Los Angeles County Museum of Art

The painting depicts the tribunal of a young nun who is seduced into leaving the convent by Lord Marmion, a handsome but eventually faithless suitor. Rosenthal's focal point is upon the tense courtroom drama at the moment that the monks yank away Constance's cloak from her shoulders to reveal she is dressed as Lord Marmion's page.

In the background towards the right two monks cheerfully prepare the niche where she will be bricked-up alive for breaking her religious vows.

$\mathcal{P}$epe's $\mathcal{S}$hroud

A Graveyard Story

Appeared in *The Argonaut*, October 16, 1886

$\mathcal{P}$epe Murhua was perhaps the most popular young man in San Felipe. He was a singularly cheery lad, and to his unfailing good spirits, no doubt, owed much of his popularity, rather than to his many qualities of greater sterling worth. But the trait which excited most interest among his compeers of his own age and sex was his dauntless, daring courage. None so reckless as Pepe when the amateurs took the bullring for some *función* whose funds were devoted to charitable or patriotic purposes; none pushed his horse to such strenuous efforts, nor clung so persistently to the game at the *coleadero* when the young bloods of the community pitted their strength one against another in "tailing the bull." And brave he was, too, in emergencies in which the soul is less highly keyed to heroism than in such stimulating phases of dash and enthusiasm. Facing calmly and in cold blood men maddened by drink or passion, or else turning a bold, defiant front to the lawless gentry infesting, in his day, the district, Pepe demonstrated ever his self-possession and courageous spirit.

A group of Pepe's friends had had his attributes under discussion, one flawy, flighty Sunday afternoon, when the sudden intermittent gusts of rain and the dusty wind had driven them to shelter from the rather bleak alameda, where to-day no carriages dashed under the garrulous cottonwoods, nor demure dark-eyed maidens paced the graveled ways or perched, like gay birds, upon the massive stucco benches. The coterie had betaken themselves to the house of Don Enrique Soto, at the instance of Federico, his son, who sat brimming their glasses with the cordial wine of Parras—to the disdain, be it admitted, of divers supercilious spirits, who would have been vastly better contented with any poor, thin liquor, so only that it should bear a foreign label.

"I tell you, comrades all," cried Pablo Núñez, "this fine fellow Pepe gets credit for valor he does not know. In all these feats of strength that he performs he knows he is at an advantage by virtue of his limber build and strong muscles. But the true test of courage will be a case where he is on equality with others—with all the world. How would he behave during an earthquake, when his tremendous strength would avail him nothing? How long would he stand up before an intangible shape—a phantom?

At that a shouted chorus of laughter ascended from the circle of young men.

"*¡Por Dios!* Pablo, dost thou believe in phantoms? But what ghosts hast thou seen? Come, tell us a tale—a story—a legend. A pretty business this—that Pablo has grown credulous of ghosts—he who was wont to scoff at aught that he could not touch, regarding the doctrines of the church even as the superstitious dreams of ignorant women. Ho, Pepe!" cried the merry crew, deriding as the favorite came to the door, "here is meat for thy mirth! Here is Pablo grown superstitious!"

Pepe smiled when the babbling spirits explained the situation, not failing, either, to mark the point that the question had arisen through Núñz's doubt of Pepe's valor. But smile although he did, Pepe looked serious, too.

"Remember, mates," he said, "that Pablo is from the Sierra, and in the mountains one grows up more inclined to belief in unearthly things—the very influences of Nature, unchanged by the arts of man, tend that way."

"¡Ey ! ¡Pepe to the defense!"

"Well, yes, then," said Pepe; "and I do think, moreover, that deep down in every human heart there lurks belief, of less or greater strength, in the supernatural. Some stake their faith on dreams, and some on signs and tokens. Thou, Corvera, didst shiver and leave off playing *mallila*, one night last week, because Juan Luna came and looked over your shoulder with his crossed eyes. How many of you will join me to-morrow in a dinner I will give at twelve? Come, speak up, boys! You shall have the fullest spread the town affords, and French wines all. ¡What! ¿Are you bashful?"

No man made exuberant haste to accept Murhua's offer to make one of the thirteen; rather, the young blows looked abashed and guilty.

"¡Aja!" cried Pablo Núñez, "I told them you'd wear the white plume on some charges. Now, see, Pepe, you rank as the pluckiest fellow in town; will you go to Campo Santo alone at night?"

"I don't think I am the pluckiest," said Pepe; "there's Juan Carrazco, who faced and threw a mad bull that was charging a crowd in the market-place; and Tito Redona, who overcame and tied crazy Sanchez, the butcher, over the dead body of the maniac's son, that he had just murdered."

"So you want to dodge the trial by shifting the honors?" said Núñez, tauntingly. "These are all cases where the danger was clear and definite. You will not go to the graveyard?"

"Oh, yes," said Pepe, "I am not given to dodging; I will go. Now, mind you, I am afraid. Yes, comrades, it is true. The unknown is always the thing fullest of horrors, and I find an awful terror in the thought that, as a bare possibility, even, somewhat that is gruesome and fearful might befall. But to my mind the truest courage lies, not in our reckless, foolhardy exploits, but in fearing a thing and facing it all the same. Come, what do you wish me to do?"

"Let us go now to Campo Santo, and see what shall be the test;" and at the word they trooped out and up the street to the dreary graveyard, facing on a forlorn empty square above the alameda, a spot so desolate and forbidding that its mere contemplation would make world-weary humanity willing to cling to life rather than face the destiny of lying in such repellant confines. Death, the Reaper, had garnered ample harvests at San Felipe; his granary was full to overflowing. The long, whitewashed façade was topped by a cross above the great portal of the *zaguán*, inexplicably wide, since no carriage nor beast of burden ever crossed the threshold. In the long, narrow vestibule, or porch, a chapel was arranged, where, night and day, a lamp burned before a pictured Holy Family, and its flame threw uncanny reflections upon a row of gleaming ashen-white skulls ranged below. Passing through this species of *atrium*, the young men, sobered by their surroundings, entered the city of the dead. The graves lay thick as grass-blades, literally overlapping, and almost without exception facing westward. No shrubs, no flowers or trees enlivened the scene; only the debris of dried bouquets from the annual decoration on All Souls' Day, which had fallen a fortnight previous, and here and there a harsh, glaring wreath of yellow and black immortelles. Some of the monuments were stately and handsome, but the majority were flat, low-lying stones, carved with no particular skill or taste, and often with defective orthography. Some of the humbler sorts were built of masonry, and painted in crudest, vividest tones of blue or green, picked out with weather-tarnished gilding. A fair proportion of the monuments bore the letters "D. P.," which indicated the right of the tenants to slumber there undisturbed in perpetuity, instead of suffering exhumation like the less-favored, whose moldering bones, at the end of four or five years, would be unearthed and thrown into the common receptacle of the *huesario*.

So depressing was the place that the visitors, as with one accord, and an instinct of self-defense, lighted fresh cigarettes, and puffed vigorously, until they created a cloud of fragrant blue smoke to mingle with the murky atmosphere. They picked their way with what reverence of tread they might to a section of the northern wall, where the plaster was crumbling away from the brown adobes, while here and there in the scarred expanse were tablets bearing beside, name and date, the legend, "Slain by the Savages," in mournful suggestion of the days, not so long gone by, when the Indians had been wont to swoop in fierce raids into the city's very streets.

Then Núñez, still acting as spokesman, turned to Pepe.

"Wilt thou come here at midnight and drive a nail into this wall?"

"I will do it," answered Pepe," but with reluctance, as you know."

Then, after the inevitable chatter and chaff, the crowd lounged homeward.

It was perhaps ten o'clock when they reassembled at Pablo Núñez's office, deeming it indiscreet to start such undertaking from the *salon de billar* or any more public point. Pepe looked a little pale and eerie, but nevertheless came gallantly forward. At the last, Clemente Allande, Pepe's bosom friend, tried to dissuade him from the enterprise.

"'Tis a rash and useless thing, *hombre*. Give it up. If aught were to be gained by the going, *¡vaya!* But to gratify the jealous malice of an envious soul like Pablo, why shouldst thou risk thy life? For at night the exhalations from the graves are more than ever noxious, and thou mayest get typhus or heaven knows what from breathing them."

The plea was potent with Pepe, who had all the usual horror which Mexicans feel for the air of night, never stirring abroad after dusk without muffling his mouth and nostrils in the folds of a silken handkerchief, through which he breathed. But—"I can not recede now," he said; "cease to dissuade me, Clemente. It may be that the example will be salutary. Seeing that I undertake, for the sake of reason and courage, a thing I dislike and fear, the boys may perhaps be impelled to act with less absolute obedience to their own preferences. We Mexicans of the younger generation are a selfish lot. Give me the hammer," he added, turning back to the others, as he threw the point of his cloak over his shoulder. This wrap of Pepe's was one of his whims—an affectation, said the malicious. But it was not that. The intense patriotism of the young fellow made him cling to the long Spanish cape of his forefathers—surely the most graceful garment a man can wear—while his comrades disported themselves in overcoats or ulsters of the latest French or English cut.

Throwing then over his shoulder one long end of his *capa*, and tucking under its drooping folds the hammer and the big clumsy spike, Pepe stepped away in the darkness, up the gloomy street between the low houses, whose dark forbidding façades gave no promise of the kindly hospitality to be found within.

"He is gone," said Clemente Allande, reentering the house. "I saw him turn the corner of `The Green Devil.' "

"You should not have watched him out of sight," said one of the young men; "that brings evil fortune."

"Now, croak, you!" snapped Clemente, viciously, in the stress of his nervous foreboding, and went out to stand alone in the chilled patio, more and more deploring Pepe's undertaking. "And I might have prevented it, if I had not been a fool," he muttered; "what were easier than to have sent a hint to the *Jefatura*, and the prefect would have so moved that the guard of the graveyard would have missed his stolen key, and watch would have been kept. Better that Pepe should pay a *multa* or even take a turn in the lock-up, rather than get diphtheria or typhus in the miasmas among the graves! Then the others came out laughing, and dragged him into the card-table, where still he would not play, but sat glowering at the game.

An hour went by, another half, two hours, and Allande could bear it no longer, but sprang to his feet with an oath of disturbance.

"Two hours and Pepe not here! Some evil has assailed him! We must go to his relief."

"And find him snugly in bed," sneered Pablo Núñez; "he has been home an hour, or—*¿quien sabe?*—perhaps he was not so scrupulous as to go to the graveyard at all!"

"It does not particularly become you, Núñez, to sneer and throw aspersions on Pepe's courage, when it is at your instigation he has gone into this absurd and useless adventure. It might be interesting to seek a cause for your pique against him!"

"One need not go far for that," murmured another of the young men; "only down to the corner of Guadalupe, where Aurelia Miramontez lives."

"At all events," said Clemente, "I shall go to Pepe. You who will, may come. However, I have no faith in ghosts, and I can go alone."

But the crowd were fairly shamed by Allande's spirit, and, moved by self reproach, and, also, no doubt, by curiosity, they trooped out with him, barring only Núñez, who slunk away to his bed. The graveyard paths were dismal in their stark bareness, that left the palpable darkness unrelieved, and pressing like material substance on the pilgrims.

The leader stopped short as he rounded a tall and massive monument that concealed the particular space of the wall where their quest lay. Something undoubtedly was there, a denser concrete shape against the formless blackness of the night and the shadows from the wall. Something, too, in human semblance, and in the uncertain light shed by the lantern's flame, flickering and waving in the riotous gale, it seemed to struggle and writhe, as if in mortal throes, or else in the strain of combat. Clemente dashed forward with one wild cry.

"Pepe! oh, Pepe! To the rescue!"

He reached the spot and but one figure was there; bowing and swaying, bending and reeling in fantastic movement, as if wrestling with its own shadow, projected in grotesque, unearthly proportions upon the wall. Clemente threw his arms about the other's waist, and strove to restrain and to drag him aside. A passive and inert but powerful resistance was the result. By this time the others had gathered around, and one of them threw the lantern's rays full on Pepe Murhua's face. Then a cry of fear and horror went up from all throats, so ghastly was that pallid countenance, set in the rigid lines of mortal agony and despair.

"Will you not help to free him?" cried Clemente. "Are you all paralyzed? Come! see what holds him, so I can lay him down! I think he is grasping something on the wall."

But none of the panic-stricken crew would move, and Clemente himself, still supporting the other, sought to reach along the rigid arms, to detach them from their hold. Both arms flung free; one stiffened hand still held the heavy hammer. Then, with a sudden light breaking on his mind, the faithful Clemente caught at the folds of the ample Spanish cape, flapping and waving airily in the wind, and tried to tear them away from the form of his friend. The resistance which he encountered confirmed his belief, that had taken shape tardily, thanks to the dim and shifting, uneven light.

With a few words of explanation which deprived the incident of its supernatural aspect, he rallied his stiffened companions, prompt enough to act where only material forces were concerned. The nature of the occurrence was plain. Blown by the fitful wind, the folds of Pepe's cloak had been pierced by the heavy spike, whose broad, flat head had effectually held the strong cloth and pinned the young man to the wall. Alone there in the night with such awesome circumstance of time and place, the conditions had unbalanced his judgment when he had seemed to find himself in the grasp of Something, unseen, unknown. Nor had the poor lad succumbed to fear alone. The family physician of the Murhuas had long ago diagnosed a weakness of the heart, brought on or aggravated by Pepe's prowess in field sports, and any excess of mental or spiritual emotion must have resulted fatally. The knowledge of his condition had been kept from Pepe, with a view to averting the fate that enlightenment might have spared him.

He was buried near the spot where death had met him, but his name is not forgotten. The graceful fashion of the Spanish cloak is coming into favor again in Mexico, but never can be found a youth of San Felipe who will don the garment that is known as "the shroud of Pepe Murhua."

Chihuahua, September, 1886.

Yda H. Addis

Addis's Note: I remember my grandmother telling me a similar legend, as happening in Kentucky, with a girl for the chief actor, who became insane from the fright. It may be this is a bit of the folk-lore common to all nations; it may be that history repeats itself. I have told here the story as related to me, as of actual occurrence in Chihuahua.

Y. H. A.

Yours truly,

Yda Addis